AROUND CHI-TOWN

January: we all know the Connelly family is the closest thing the Windy City has to royalty—in fact, Emma Rosemere Connelly is actually descended from the former king of Altaria. This reporter's sources say that Emma's firstborn, Daniel, is taking family duty seriously and will shortly assume the throne in that picturesque island kingdom.

We all agree that Daniel is the catch of Chicago—rich, handsome and sexy. And honorable, too. But just who is that sweet young thing with the exotic accent who's been spotted on his arm lately by yours truly? Come on, ladies, this may be the last chance for one of *us* to become Mrs. King Daniel.

FYI, the Connellys deny these royal reports, but they're rallying around their golden boy. Just what's going on, Dapper Dan? Your secret's safe with me....

Dear Reader,

Ring in the New Year with the hottest new love stories from Silhouette Desire! *The Redemption of Jefferson Cade* by BJ James is our MAN OF THE MONTH. In this latest installment of MEN OF BELLE TERRE, the youngest Cade overcomes both external and internal obstacles to regain his lost love. And be sure to read the launch book in Desire's first yearlong continuity series, DYNASTIES: THE CONNELLYS. In *Tall, Dark & Royal*, bestselling author Leanne Banks introduces a prominent Chicago family linked to European royals.

Anne Marie Winston offers another winner with *Billionaire Bachelors: Ryan*, a BABY BANK story featuring twin babies. In *The Tycoon's Temptation* by Katherine Garbera, a jaded billionaire discovers the greater rewards of love, while Kristi Gold's *Dr. Dangerous* discovers he's addicted to a certain physical therapist's personal approach to healing in this launch book of Kristi's MARRYING AN M.D. miniseries. And Metsy Hingle bring us *Navy SEAL Dad*, a BACHELORS & BABIES story.

Start the year off right by savoring all six of these passionate, powerful and provocative romances from Silhouette Desire!

Enjoy!

Joan Marlow Golan

Joan Marlow Golan
Senior Editor, Silhouette Desire

Please address questions and book requests to:
Silhouette Reader Service
U.S.: 3010 Walden Ave., P.O. Box 1325, Buffalo, NY 14269
Canadian: P.O. Box 609, Fort Erie, Ont. L2A 5X3

Tall, Dark & Royal
LEANNE BANKS

Silhouette®

Desire.

Published by Silhouette Books

America's Publisher of Contemporary Romance

Special thanks and acknowledgment are given
to Leanne Banks for her contribution to the
DYNASTIES: THE CONNELLYS series.

 SILHOUETTE BOOKS

ISBN 0-373-76412-X

TALL, DARK & ROYAL

Visit Silhouette at www.eHarlequin.com

Printed in U.S.A.

Books by Leanne Banks

LEANNE BANKS

is a national number-one bestselling author of romance. She lives in her native Virginia with her husband, son and daughter. Recognized for both her sensual and humorous writing with two Career Achievement Awards from *Romantic Times Magazine,* Leanne likes creating a story with a few grins, a generous kick of sensuality and characters who hang around after the book is finished. Leanne believes romance readers are the best readers in the world because they understand that love is the greatest miracle of all. You can contact Leanne online at leannebbb@aol.com or write to her at P.O. Box 1442, Midlothian, VA 23113. A SASE for a reply would be greatly appreciated.

MEET THE CONNELLYS

Wealthy, Powerful and Rocked by Scandal,
Betrayal...and Passion!

Who's Who in *Tall, Dark & Royal*

In Chicago:

Daniel Connelly—He loves basketball, Chicago hot dogs
and his privacy. How will he ever be king of Altaria?

Erin Lawrence—She teaches Daniel royal etiquette...but
exactly what does this young, unawakened woman want to
learn from Daniel...?

Emma Rosemere Connelly—The former princess of Altaria
left the palace on the arm of her upstart American husband
thirty-five years ago...and hasn't looked back.

Grant Connelly—The family patriarch has amassed a
fortune and enriched his offspring with life's true riches:
honor, duty and loyalty.

Brett Connelly—Can Daniel take advice from his glib
playboy brother?

Maggie Connelly—The baby of the family and a free spirit,
she loves modern art and fast cars.

In Altaria:

Mr. Lawrence—Erin's father, the foreign minister, doesn't
want Daniel to be king. But how far will he go to stop it?

Gregor Paulus—The palace aide's manners are impeccable
and his bearing regal.

Anthony Muller—Chief of staff at the palace, he keeps on
the staff's back and on Daniel's good side.

Prologue

Merry Christmas. You're the new ruler of Altaria, his mother might as well have said.

The snow fell outside the window of Daniel Connelly's Chicago high-rise condominium as he tried to make sense of his mother's announcement. Not every man in America had a mother who was a former princess. Although she'd always been Mom to Daniel, and she'd given up her title thirty-five years ago when she'd married his father, Emma Rosemere Connelly had never lost the regal poise drilled into her by years spent as Princess of Altaria. Even now, faced with the news that her father and brother had been killed in a boating accident, she held herself together as she sat beside her husband on the brown leather couch.

"You're going to have to repeat that, Mom," Daniel said, sinking into his favorite chair.

His mother took his hands in hers and leaned toward him intently. Her cold fingers and the glint of pain in her blue eyes betrayed her emotions. She gave a sad smile. "I've told you many stories about Altaria. You've even visited a couple of times."

Daniel nodded, his mind filling with vague childhood memories. "I remember Altaria as a beautiful island off the coast of Italy with a great beach," he said. "But how in the world can I be its new ruler?"

"Altarian law stipulates that only male descendants can assume the throne. My father and brother are dead," she said, and squeezed his hands in a moment of telltale grief. Out of the corner of his eye, Daniel saw his father squeeze his mother's shoulders in a gesture of support. Grant Connelly had made his fortune in textiles, but his backbone was made of steel. His mother took a quick breath. "My brother had only one daughter, Catherine. He had no male children."

Daniel thought about some of the gossip he'd heard about his uncle, Prince Marc, over the years. "I don't want to speak ill of the dead, but are you sure Uncle Marc didn't have any other children? He really seemed to take that playboy-prince role to heart."

His father made a sound between a cough and chuckle.

His mother frowned. "Daniel," she said, her tone just a shade sharper. "Marc may have had his flaws, but he would never turn his back on his own child. You are the heir to the throne of Altaria."

Daniel's head reeled. In all his thirty-four years, he'd never imagined being a ruler of a small kingdom. Chicago-born and -bred, he'd always assumed he would spend his life in America. He glanced at his father, a man who had taken the family textile company and turned it into a Fortune 500 corporation. His father had always possessed a passion for the family business, an unrelenting zeal to make it grow.

Daniel had not.

He had succeeded in competitive sports in college, and he had succeeded as Vice President of Marketing at Connelly Corporation, but he'd always had the sense that something was missing, that he wanted something deeper, more. Could this possibly be it?

King? Lord help him.

He looked at his parents and shook his head. *"King?"*

His father nodded and leaned forward. "You've got what it takes to lead a country if that's what you think you should do. It's your choice."

His mother squeezed his hand again. She looked at him with a mixture of pride and concern in her eyes. "Consider it carefully. My father had such dreams for Altaria. When he founded the Rosemere Institute to research cancer treatment, he not only provided a beautiful memorial to my mother, he also brought Altaria into the scientific age. Ruling will be a heavy responsibility, and once you start down this road, your life will be changed forever."

One

She was late, but anxious to meet her assignment. Erin Lawrence bit her lip at her slip. *Begin* her assignment, she mentally corrected. His Majesty might not appreciate being regarded as an assignment. Even if that were true.

She adjusted her hat, then showed her identification to the security guard on the bottom floor of Daniel Connelly's high-rise condominium. Despite the jet lag from her delayed flight, she felt a rush of anticipation as she entered the steel elevator. Even though she'd arrived at night, she couldn't help noticing how different Chicago's architecture was from the Mediterranean-style houses and buildings in her homeland, Altaria.

The elevator doors whisked open, and she walked down the hallway to Daniel Connelly's condo. She lifted her hand to ring the buzzer, and her heart hammered in her chest. Taking a deep breath, she couldn't escape the sense of history surrounding this moment. She was about to meet the royal heir to the throne of Altaria.

Squaring her shoulders, she pressed her index finger into the buzzer and waited.

And waited. A dog barked in the background.

She counted to twenty, then pushed the buzzer again and waited. The dog continued to bark.

The door opened and a tall man with tousled hair and jade-green eyes met her gaze. His chest was bare and muscular, and the only item of clothing he wore was a pair of lounging slacks slung low on his narrow hips. "You rang?"

"Perhaps I'm at the wrong—" She broke off, totally fixated on his wide shoulders and all that naked skin. A dusting of chest hair arrowed down to the top of his slacks. Leaning against the doorjamb with indolent ease, he gave the impression that he was comfortable with his half-naked body. Something told Erin he knew his way around a woman's naked body. This was the kind of man all her headmistresses had warned her against. This was the kind of man who inspired all the bad girls to sneak out of their windows at night.

Tearing her gaze from his impressive body, Erin rechecked the number on his door. The address was correct. She swallowed over a knot of apprehension. "Your Majesty?" she said weakly.

His gaze cleared, and he lifted his head in realization. "You must be Erin Lawrence, the royal etiquette rep."

"Royal etiquette and palace liaison," she said, fighting a twinge of irritation at his casual description of her position. She gave a slight dip. "At your service, sir."

His gaze swept over her in brief masculine assessment that hinted at banked, yet powerful sensuality. She held her breath, until he looked into her eyes again with a glint of amusement. "For some reason I thought you were supposed to arrive earlier today."

"Yes, of course, sir. I apologize. My flights were delayed."

"Happens to everyone," he said generously and held the door for her to enter. "Come on in. Sorry I'm not dressed for the occasion. I had nine meetings today, so I decided to hit the sack early. Don't worry about the dog. I put Jordan in his kennel when I answered the door," he said, referring to the barking dog.

"Jordan, sir?"

"In honor of Michael Jordan, the best basketball player the Chicago Bulls were sorry to lose."

Erin made a mental note to bone up on American basketball. She knew nothing about it. She stopped midway through the doorway and gazed expectantly at him. "The rule of protocol is the king should precede, sir. One should never turn one's back to the king."

"Oh." He gave her another once-over. "Well, that could be a damn shame."

Erin felt a rush of heat to her cheeks and prayed he didn't notice. "Please do proceed, sir. I will follow."

He gave a slow nod, then led the way through a luxurious living room furnished with contemporary brown leather furniture and oak end tables. She followed him into a clean, well-equipped kitchen. He opened the refrigerator door and pulled out a carton of milk. "You want something to drink? Or a sandwich?"

The man was almost completely unaware of his position, she thought, and wondered how he would change once he began to exercise his power as king. *If* he exercised his power as king. Daniel Connolly struck her as a man who didn't need a title or decree. Staring at his wide shoulders, she caught her mind wandering and gave herself a mental shake. The king was offering to fix her a drink or a sandwich. That would never do. "No, thank you, sir."

He grimaced slightly. "Do you mind me asking how old you are?"

She stiffened her spine. "Twenty-two, sir."

"You're young, but we're both adults. Do you have to call me sir?"

"It's proper, sir," she said.

He sighed. "Okay," he said and took a swig directly from the milk carton.

Erin's eyes widened in horror.

He must have caught her expression because he gave her a grin. "Don't worry. Last sip," he told her and tossed the empty carton into the trash container.

Erin practiced what had been drilled into her from years at the finest Swiss boarding schools: she kept her mouth shut. This was the new king of Altaria—a good-looking American who had a body that would make any woman's temperature shoot up ten degrees and who clearly had zero knowledge about royal protocol. She wondered how many of his Altarian ancestors would be spinning in their graves.

Heaven help Altaria.

Heaven help her.

"I'm not exactly sure what your role is," he said.

"I'm to fill you in on royal protocol and also to learn as much about your preferences as possible so that the palace is well prepared for your arrival, sir."

He raked his hand through his hair. "Translate *royal protocol.*"

"Traditional royal etiquette, sir. It's my job to inform you about how the people of Altaria will greet you and how you will be expected to respond."

He sighed again and rubbed his hand over his face. "Etiquette lessons. I'll have to fit them in sometime after an airport expansion plan and a budget review. How about if you take a couple of days to take care of your jet lag and we can get together then?"

"I'm quite able to perform my duties immediately, sir."

"Tell you what, get settled and we'll talk tomorrow or the next day."

Erin felt as if she was getting the brush-off. That wouldn't do. Her father, the foreign minister of Altaria, had assigned her this job—in spite of her unfortunate nervous response that had been the bane of her existence as long as she could remember. She couldn't fail her father. This was her opportunity to forge a closer relationship with him. "I can be useful to you, sir. My father is Altaria's foreign minister, so I'm quite familiar with the political climate."

Daniel Connelly gave her a considering glance. "Okay. I'll call you after I get through the most critical matters. Welcome to the Windy City." At her puzzled look, he clarified, "Welcome to Chicago."

"Thank you, sir."

"Are you sure you don't want something to drink?"

His insistent hospitality disconcerted her. "Quite sure, sir. Thank you."

He nodded and picked up a phone. "Then I'll tell security to get you a cab."

"Oh, that's not necessary, sir. I can do that."

"I'm sure you can, but *my* protocol won't allow me to send a young lady visitor out into the streets of Chicago without transportation to her destination."

A gentleman? A secret warmth slid through her. She'd been surrounded by so many men more concerned with their own self-importance that she almost didn't know how to respond. "Thank you, sir," she murmured as he gave instructions to the security attendant.

Daniel led her to the door and opened it for her. "Why does your accent sound British?" he asked.

"Although I attended Swiss boarding schools, the headmistresses were British."

"Your bearing is similar to my mother's," he said.

"I take that as high praise, sir," she said. "I attended the same boarding school she did years earlier. Princess Emma has always been much beloved and admired by the people of Altaria."

"Even though she gave up her title to marry a rough American upstart?" he asked with a sly, yet appealing grin.

"She may have officially given up her title as princess, sir, but she is always a princess in the hearts of Altarians."

He chuckled. "You're very good. Are you sure you're not a public relations specialist?"

"Knowledge of public relations is required for my position, sir. As I told you, however, part of my job is to learn what pleases you so you will feel at home in Altaria.''

"I'm not hard to please. A Bulls game and a Chicago hot dog, and I'm happy.''

Erin blinked, trying to imagine the palace chef preparing a Chicago hot dog. Whatever it was. "I'll make note of it, sir.''

"I'm sure you will. Good night.''

Daniel winced as he listened to his voice mail messages two days later. Three of them were from Erin Lawrence. He remembered what a prim but curvy little package she'd been. She was so proper, his contrary mind couldn't resist visualizing her stripped of her perfect manners and clothes. Daniel had also noticed, however, that while Miss Lawrence was a babe, she also gave the impression of innocence, forbidden fruit.

He hadn't deliberately pushed her aside, but his transition from Vice President of Marketing at Connelly Corporation to King of Altaria had him swamped. To ensure continuity of succession, the successor to a monarch was normally required to be present immediately, so it seemed odd that the foreign minister had told Daniel they weren't quite ready for him yet. Daniel decided to bide his time with his questions. He had plenty to do with the loose ends he had to tie up in Chicago and the preparations he needed to make for Altaria.

Glancing at his packed-to-the-brim schedule on

his electronic organizer, he saw that dinner was clear and punched out the telephone number for Erin's hotel. "Daniel Connelly here," he said when she answered the phone.

"Thank you for calling, Your Majesty," she said in a proper, but well-modulated tone. Daniel wondered what it would take to ruffle her perfect poise. He wondered what kind of underwear she wore, but pushed the thought aside.

"Sorry it took so long. I've been swamped, and today's not much better. Can you join me for dinner? I'll order pizza and we can meet at my place."

A long paused followed.

"Problem?"

"No, sir," she said, her voice clearly reluctant.

"I hear 'problem' in your voice, Miss Lawrence," he said, feeling a twitch of impatience. "What is it?"

"I'm just trying to determine the propriety of my giving you a protocol lesson in your private quarters, sir," she replied.

"Didn't you tell me earlier that you wanted privacy?" he asked.

"Yes, sir, but—"

"Do you need a chaperone or something?"

"Absolutely not, sir," she said with a trace of defiance in her voice. "I'll meet you for dinner. What time?"

"Make it late," he said. "Seven-thirty."

"Very good sir. I'll see you at seven-thirty."

Daniel hung up the phone and groaned aloud just as the door to his office pushed open to reveal his brother, Brett.

"How's it going, YM?" Brett asked and cracked a half-grin. "The king stuff getting to you already?"

Daniel threw his brother a dark look. "YM?"

"Short for Your Majesty," Brett said. "The press is sniffing around big-time. They all want an interview, but I should be able to hold them off a little longer."

Born with a silver tongue, Brett had been the perfect choice for Vice President of Public Relations for Connelly Corporation. He not only reveled in the ability to work the press to the advantage of Connelly Corporation, he also enjoyed his single playboy status to the max—something Daniel had grown weary of during the past couple of years.

"You think Justin is ready for the world of marketing?" Brett asked.

Their straitlaced brother Justin was steady and responsible and more than willing to climb the Connelly Corporation corporate ladder. "Justin will do a great job replacing me or he'll die trying," he said.

"All of us will miss you, but—"

"—but don't let the door hit me on my way out," Daniel said with a wry chuckle. Whether the game was sports or business, there'd always been a friendly combination of camaraderie and competition among the Connelly males.

"You've done a terrific job," Brett said. "Don't

get me wrong. But I always got the impression you wanted something different. You think this is it?''

Surprised at his brother's insight, Daniel nodded. ''It's got to be. I have to believe fate is at work here. I always wanted to make a difference, not necessarily in the textile world.''

''Those Altarians are damn lucky to get you,'' Brett said.

''I don't know about that. I get the feeling the foreign minister isn't dying for me to move in. He's been slow to send information I've requested, but he did send his daughter,'' Daniel said, unable to mask a slight grimace.

''Daughter? What for?''

''Royal protocol.''

Brett blinked, then barked with laughter. ''She's going to try to teach you everything you tried not to learn from Mom.''

''And more, I'm sure,'' Daniel said, and waved his hand. ''I really don't have time for this right now, but I don't want to be rude.''

''What's she like?''

''Prim and proper,'' Daniel said, then added, ''with killer curves.''

Brett's mouth lifted in a wolfish grin. ''Then maybe there will be some fringe benefits with the lessons, after all.''

Although the prospect of intimately exploring Erin's curves tempted the hell out of him, Daniel shook his head. "I don't think so. I've never seen a woman so determined to make me perfect."

Erin juggled a large pizza box with two volumes on royal etiquette along with a photo book on royal uniforms as she twisted around to push His Majesty's buzzer with her elbow. Since the pizza had arrived at the same time she had, she'd suggested delivering it herself.

Daniel opened the door, and she was struck again by his height. His eyes widened.

"Let me help you—"

Just as he reached for the heavy books, a blur of something large and brown raced across the room and careened into her. Erin toppled toward the floor.

"Jordan, heel!" Daniel yelled, and the dog abruptly backed off.

Her knees hit the hard stone floor, and pain shot through her, but she automatically squeezed her fingers around the pizza box. Her face was going to hit the floor or the pizza box, she thought in despair, just as strong hands caught her shoulders.

Daniel swore under his breath. "I'm sorry," he said. "He smelled the pizza and went nuts. He's spooked by all the visitors that have been in and out of here over the last week."

She felt him lift her as if she were a flower. He carried her to the couch and she was acutely aware of his muscular chest pressed against her. She couldn't recall the last time she'd been carried, not even by her father. She felt an odd, but gentle stroke at a hidden tender spot inside her. It mystified her. She felt Daniel try to pry the box from her fingers.

"You can let go of the pizza now," he said, furrowing his eyebrows.

Still distracted, she felt heat rise to her cheeks. "Oh, I'm sorry, Your Majesty."

He looked at her quizzically. "I'm surprised you didn't drop it when Jordan crashed into you."

She blinked. "Training, I guess, sir. Don't lose your dignity, but if you do, don't spill your tray."

His lips twitched. "Your teacher should be proud." He set the pizza box on top of an entertainment center and turned to the dog. "No pizza for you tonight. That's no way to treat a lady," he muttered.

Erin took a long look at the contrite dog. The animal was huge, with dark soulful eyes and large paws. "I'm not sure I've ever seen that particular breed, sir," she said, unable to mask her curiosity. The beast looked like a combination of a brown bear and a bulldog.

Daniel ruffled the dog's ears. "He's a mixed breed," he said, then shot Erin a look that mixed humor and undiluted masculine sex appeal. "Mixed breed. Kinda like me. Half Altarian royalty and half American rebel," he said and led the whining dog to another room.

So true, she thought, except Daniel was much better-looking than his dog. Erin tried to collect her wits. Taking a deep breath, she wasn't sure which had rattled her more, the dog rushing her or Daniel carrying her to the couch. Her books, she suddenly remembered, reining in her strange feelings. Focus on the job, she told herself, not His Majesty's distracting body. Glancing toward the doorway, she saw the books on the floor. Daniel must have dropped them to catch her.

She moved her legs to rise from the sofa and felt a twinge. She looked down at her stockings. They were shredded and one of her legs was scratched and slightly bleeding.

Daniel returned to the room at that very moment. He swore again and rushed toward her, then bent down and gingerly touched her leg. "Damn. I'll get some antiseptic and a bandage."

Flustered, Erin shook her head. "That's not necessary," she said to his back as he strode from the room. She jumped to her feet to follow him. "Sir, this is not at all proper protocol," she protested, but might as well have been talking to the dog for all the attention Daniel was paying her. As he entered the bathroom, she paused outside the door, uncertain what to do next.

She watched him collect some items from the medicine cabinet and run some water over a washcloth. He turned to face her. "Go back to the sofa," he said, meeting her with a gaze that said he meant business.

"But, sir—"

"But nothing," he returned, striding past her. "My dog did this to you. I'm responsible."

Distressed, she followed him into the living room again and resumed her seat on the sofa. "Sir, this truly is not appropriate."

"What would be appropriate? For me to order a servant to take care of your scratch?"

"Yes, sir, or I could do it myself."

He shook his head and knelt in front of her. "Neither of those choices work for me. I'm king, I'm pulling rank." He glanced at her leg, then met her gaze. "You need to ditch your stockings."

Erin's heart climbed into her throat. Seeing the unswerving determination in his eyes, she held her breath for a full moment. She opened her mouth and closed it, then cleared her throat. "Could you please turn around, sir?" she asked in a voice that sounded high-pitched to her own ears.

Realization crossed his face. He shrugged. "Sure. Let me know when you're ready."

Try never, sir, she thought, as she pushed her stockings down her legs with unsteady hands. The horrified face of her finishing-school teacher flashed before her eyes. Erin had known this assignment would be challenging, but she'd never imagined finding herself in such an awkward position. Stepping out of her pumps, she pulled the shredded hose off her feet and tried again to collect herself.

"Ready?" he asked as if he had eyes in the back of his head.

"Yes, sir," she said reluctantly.

He turned around and lifted his hands just above her knee to the scraped place on her leg. Her leg automatically stiffened. His gaze shot up to meet hers. "Sore?"

"A little, I suppose, sir," she managed, too aware of the fact that His Majesty was kneeling before her. She felt the threat of her dreaded secret nervous response and closed her eyes. She took slow, soothing breaths and pictured a peaceful Swiss snowfall.

An odd intimacy seemed to swim between them when he touched her thigh. His hands were gentle as he cleaned the scrape and applied antibiotic ointment. He put on the bandage and Erin opened her eyes. She caught him looking at her painted toenails.

She couldn't resist the urge to curl her toes into the carpet.

He skimmed his hand down her leg to her feet, sending an odd ripple through her. "These are going to get cold. I can give you some socks," he offered, rising to his feet.

He looked down at her and held her gaze for a long moment in which the world seemed to turn on its axis. Erin held her breath. She watched his gaze dip to her lips for several heart-stopping seconds before he glanced away. Briefly, he shook his head, almost as if he'd considered kissing her, then come to his senses.

Erin wondered when she would come to *her* senses.

"Socks," he muttered. "They may not make the kind of fashion statement you usually make, but you'll be more comfortable." He narrowed his eyes. "Come to think of it, you're not going to want to go back to your hotel with bare legs. I'll get you a pair of sweatpants and a sweatshirt."

Erin felt a rush of panic. Wearing His Majesty's clothes? How had this situation gotten so totally beyond her control? "Thank you very much, sir, but it's truly not necessary."

"Of course it is," he said. "It's January in Chicago. No one in their right mind faces the elements with bare skin," he said, then his eyes glinted with masculine intensity. "Although it's a damn shame to cover legs as nice as yours with sweatpants."

Erin's heart skipped over itself, and a rush of emotions swam through her. How was she supposed to accomplish her job, maintain appropriate distance and, as her father had requested, subtly discourage Daniel from accepting the throne, when Daniel was clearly determined to treat her as a human being more than as a protocol instructor? How, in heaven's name, was she supposed to maintain her equilibrium when this man emanated enough electrical energy to burn her to a crisp?

Two

As Erin sat on Daniel's couch, it occurred to her that it was tough to remain proper and starchy when she was wearing a sweat suit that swallowed her. She stiffened her back. "I brought several books for your reference, sir," she said. "This one is the most complete. I have another on royal etiquette, and I brought a book with pictures of the military uniforms you'll wear for a variety of occasions. Some people absorb information more easily if it's introduced in a visual manner."

Daniel thumbed through one of the books and gave her a considering glance. "You thought I might need a picture book?"

Oops. She hoped she hadn't insulted his intelligence. "With all the information you're being given, sir, I thought it might be easier if some of it weren't delivered to you in such a dry manner."

One side of his lips lifted in a half grin. "I'm curious what you've been told about me."

Erin sifted through half a dozen things her father had told her that couldn't be repeated. "I know you're thirty-four years old and you are Vice President of Marketing for the Connelly Corporation, sir. I've been told you attended college with a football scholarship and you're as American as—" She searched her brain for the correct term. "As popcorn," she said. "Or is it pie?"

He flashed his teeth in a grin. "Both will do."

"The most important thing, sir, is that you are the eldest son of Princess Emma, which makes you the natural heir to the Altarian throne. And you are consenting to relinquish your life as an American to serve as King of Altaria."

He nodded. "Just to fill in a couple of blanks, I graduated from Northwestern with degrees in Business Administration and Philosophy. Do you have a laptop at your hotel?"

She nodded, wondering where this was leading.

He gave a careless shrug. "If you're interested, Northwestern has an informative Web site."

Erin had the uncomfortable feeling that there were quite a few gaps in the profile of Daniel she'd received. "I'll do that, sir."

Daniel glanced back at the book. "Let me get this

straight. Part of my job is to appear at various events in these military uniforms."

"Yes, sir," she said. "Traditional decorum provides a certain security for the people."

"Okay. Will there be someone at the palace who will be knowledgeable about what uniform I wear when?"

"Of course, sir. You will have at least two royal dressers at your service."

"In that case, I could safely delegate the task of whether I wear red or blue to one of the royal dressers, right?"

"I suppose, sir. I thought that since there will be a significant difference in your attire, you would prefer to be informed."

Daniel shut the book with a smile. "As long as nobody puts me in a pink tutu, I really don't give a damn." He laced his fingers together and leaned toward her. "I'd really rather know more about the people of Altaria."

Erin blinked. This definitely wasn't going as planned. Her father had instructed her that if she couldn't discourage Daniel from accepting the throne, then she needed to convince him that the position of king was more decoration than substance. "The people of Altaria, sir?"

"Yes. You're Altarian. How would you describe your people?"

"Warm and caring, sir," she said, thinking of the island people who provided services to tourists and fresh fruit and vegetables. "They're very family-oriented. Because of the isolation of the island, they're not especially sophisticated in terms of higher education."

"Why not?" he prompted.

"We have no schools of higher learning on the island, sir."

"Why not?"

"There never have been. Anyone who wants to send their children to school sends them to the continent."

Daniel frowned. "So if someone was motivated and intelligent, but their family didn't have the means to send them to a university in Europe, then they wouldn't get to go at all?"

She nodded. "Correct, sir. Such a person would likely continue to do whatever his or her father or mother did."

"And what is the parliament's stand on this?"

"The parliament is slow to change without considerable provocation."

He frowned again as if he didn't like her answer. "What do you think the people of Altaria want in a king?"

She felt a distressing tug in opposite directions. Part of her was drawn to Daniel's sincere interest in her people, while at the same time she couldn't forget her father's wishes. Erin found she could only answer him honestly. "Sir, I believe the citizens of Altaria want a king who will provide a bridge from

the past to the future. Even Americans understand
that tradition can be a source of comfort in times of
grief. Altaria takes great pride in the unbroken line
of succession the Rosemeres have provided. Altarians want a ruler who appreciates where they have
been and where they need to go.''

Daniel nodded slowly. "I guess that means I need
to bone up on Altarian history. You said you were
familiar with the political climate. How does the
parliament feel about an American taking the
throne?''

Her stomach tightened, and she glanced away.
"The official stance is that the parliament is pleased
there is a healthy heir ready and willing to take the
throne, sir. Many were surprised that you would
agree to give up your privacy and freedom to accept
the job.''

Daniel sighed and stood. He moved toward the
huge picture window and glanced out. "I don't believe in shirking family duty. My parents drilled into
all of us that we have responsibilities to fulfill. I
wouldn't be able to look myself in the mirror if I
didn't fulfill mine, but—'' He broke off and glanced
at her. "But I've always felt I was biding my time
at Connelly Corporation. God knows, I wouldn't
have chosen to be king, but it appears the job has
chosen me.'' He turned to meet her eyes, and she
felt the intensity in his gaze clear down to her toes.
"I'm a Connelly. I can't do less than my best.''

His words vibrated between them, and Erin began

to sense that there was far more to Daniel Connelly than she or her father could have imagined.

His green gaze shifted like the Chicago wind as he moved toward her. "You've told me the official position of the parliament. What's the unofficial stance?"

Erin's mind locked in panic. She needed to obey her father and follow his wishes, but... She tried to find a way to protect her father without undermining her own sense of integrity. "Unofficially and officially, the parliament embraces tradition and is very slow to change, sir."

"A nice way of saying I probably make them nervous," he said.

"I didn't say that, sir," she protested.

"You didn't have to." He cocked his head to one side. "I make you nervous, too."

Confounded was a more accurate description, she thought. "No, sir. Of course not," she said, but felt she wasn't exactly telling the truth.

"Not at all?" he asked, sitting down on the couch next to her.

Her stomach fluttered nervously at his closeness. "Well, perhaps a little, sir. You're not exactly what I expected."

"How am I different?" he asked, his gaze so intense she wondered if he could see straight through her.

Erin barely resisted the urge to squirm. "It's truly not my place to say, sir," she said.

Irritation crossed his face. "Well, I'm king, so what happens if I'd like to know?"

She bit her lip as her stomach churned. "Is that an order, sir?"

"Is that what it takes?"

"Yes, sir," she said reluctantly.

He nodded decisively. "Done. How am I different from what you expected?"

Erin took a deep breath and wished she could fly away through that huge plate-glass window. She looked away from him. "You're more intelligent than I expected, sir," she admitted in a low voice, then added an explanation. "Football scholarship."

"Northwestern is a highly competitive university. The academic requirements are high for everyone, including the football team."

"Oh," she said.

"What else?"

"You have a sense of honor that surprises me, sir. Your interest in the Altarian people is... unexpected. You are kinder and less self-absorbed than I would have imagined," she continued and took a shallow breath. Her chest felt tight with anxiety. "You look at me when I talk to you. You pay attention to what I say."

"That surprises you?" he asked.

She met his gaze and nodded silently.

"Why would I not pay attention to what you say?" he asked.

She shrugged and thought of how many times

she'd felt that her father looked past her instead of at her. "I don't know sir. I guess I'm just not accustomed to it."

He frowned thoughtfully for a moment, then met her eyes again. "What else?"

Erin had the frightful urge yet again to fidget. She clenched her hands together in her lap. "You are taller, sir," she said. And better looking, she thought, but she refused to utter those words.

"What's the height of the average Altarian man?" he asked.

"I don't know, sir. Shorter than you."

He chuckled. "How have I not surprised you?"

Erin's stomach tightened with dread. "Is that an order, sir?"

He nodded and cracked a grin. "Yeah."

"You are very American, very casual, and you couldn't be less interested in learning royal protocol. Sir," she added, and relaxed. She was finished. No more honest and potentially embarrassing disclosures.

"You're right about that," he said. "To keep it fair, I'll tell you how you're different from what I expected."

Erin's stomach immediately twisted into a square knot.

"Even though I knew you were the foreign minister's daughter, I imagined you would be a lot older."

"Older, sir?" she managed.

"Around fifty with orthopedic shoes, and annoyingly prissy and proper."

His words stung. Annoyingly prissy and proper hit a bit close to home.

"Instead, you're this blue-eyed blonde with killer legs who is annoyingly prissy and proper," he said, softening his assessment with a sexy grin. "But maybe it's your job to be prissy and proper. I can't help imagining what you're like when you're not on the clock or on guard," he said, putting his hand over hers and gently prying her fingers from their locked position. "In time, maybe I'll find out."

Erin's heart stuttered. Not if she could help it.

An hour and a half later, after Erin had returned to her hotel room and scoured the Northwestern University Web site, she paced the floor of her small suite. Her phone rang and she knew immediately who it was. Her father.

"Have you met with the American?" he asked without preamble.

"Yes, I met with His Majesty tonight."

"Are you making progress with him?"

Not much, she thought, pushing her hair from her face. "I find I wasn't given adequate information about our new king," she said, unable to keep her irritation from her voice.

"What information?" her father asked.

"I was led to believe he wasn't particularly bright."

"He isn't," her father insisted. "He's a football player."

"Father, this man graduated with honors from a prestigious university." She still felt like a fool because of her wrong assumptions about Daniel.

"That doesn't qualify him to rule Altaria," her father said.

"No. The only thing that qualifies him to be King of Altaria is the fact that he is the eldest male Rosemere. He could easily be an eighteen-year-old inheriting the throne. Instead he's an intelligent, experienced thirty-four-year-old man."

"An eighteen-year-old would likely be easier to manage," her father grumbled. "Do you think you'll be able to discourage him from taking the throne?"

Erin's chest tightened with conflicting feelings. She understood some of her father's reservations about Daniel. He was an American, after all, with very little knowledge or appreciation of Altaria's history. Her father feared Daniel would move in like a bull in a china shop, disrupting the peace and tranquillity of the kingdom. Erin remembered the determined expression on Daniel's face when he talked about taking the throne. "I don't know, Father. I sense His Majesty views his role as king as an act of duty and honor."

Her father's disapproving silence stretched on, and Erin closed her eyes.

"You're not switching loyalties, are you?" he asked quietly.

"No," she said, but she wondered how she would settle the conflict tugging at her. Her father wasn't here, dealing with Daniel Connelly in the flesh. "You are my father and Altaria is my country."

"Remember, Erin, just because he is a good man doesn't mean he would be good for Altaria. Get some sleep, child. I will call again," he said and hung up.

Erin returned the phone to the cradle and stared out the window at the lights of the Chicago skyline. She hugged her arms around herself. Her father had called her child. She hadn't felt like a child for years. Her mother had died when Erin was so young that she only had vague memories of softness, gentle laughter, sweet touches and perfume.

Spending her childhood in boarding school had made her grow up quickly, forced to depend only on herself. She'd spent a lot of years hiding her loneliness. Now she finally had a chance to forge a bond with her father, and she wasn't at all sure she would be able to accomplish it.

She absently rubbed the soft fleece sweatshirt and glanced down at the too-large sweatpants she still wore. It was odd, but wearing Daniel's sweat suit made her feel as if she were wrapped in a big, warm hug. She wondered what it would be like to be wrapped in Daniel's arms. She wondered how his lips would feel on her mouth, on her skin. The thought nearly gave her hiccups.

Ridiculous, she thought, rolling her eyes at herself. She went to the bathroom to brush her teeth and tried to dismiss her unsettling thoughts about His Majesty. She chanted the title to drill it into her mind. "His Majesty, His Majesty, His Majesty," she murmured as she pulled out a nightgown and changed her clothes.

Erin immediately noticed that the big, warm hug was gone. She dashed under the covers and pulled them up over her head just as she'd done a thousand times as a child. She tried not to think about Daniel, but she couldn't forget how gently he'd touched her thigh and how he'd insisted she wear his clothes. She couldn't forget that when she talked to him, he looked at her, not past her. She couldn't forget *him*.

"I know it's short notice," Daniel said the following morning. "But if you're not doing anything tonight, would you attend the Big Brothers' charity ball tonight with me?"

Since Erin had arrived in Chicago, she hadn't been less busy in her life. She struggled to mesh her job description with Daniel's last-minute invitation. "A Big Brothers' charity ball, sir?" she echoed.

"It's one of my family's pet charities and I promised I would attend before I got the king assignment. I told my mother I would still attend as long as I can keep it low profile. In other words, we'll arrive late and leave early. Are you game?''

Her mind still reeling, Erin twisted the phone cord around her finger. ''But why me, sir?''

''There are other women I could take, but I'd spend the evening dodging any discussion of my future plans. I'm leaving this world and going into another. You're the one who understands that best.''

Flattered despite herself, Erin felt her heart swell in her chest.

''So, yes or no?''

She fought a thread of panic. ''I didn't bring anything appropriate to wear to a ball.''

''This is Chicago, a shopping Mecca,'' he said, countering her concern. ''Put what you need on my tab and make sure you get a wrap too. The ball begins at eight. I'll pick you up at eight-thirty.

''Yes, sir,'' she said, wondering which turn this roller-coaster assignment was going to take next.

Ten hours later, a knock sounded at Erin's door and her heart rate sprinted. She opened the door and her breath caught at the sight of Daniel in a black tux with a black overcoat and a white cashmere scarf. The image of the American upstart was immediately replaced with that of a sophisticated, dangerously handsome man.

His gaze trailed over her. ''You clean up very nicely, Miss Lawrence,'' he said with a sensual edge to his voice.

''Thank you, Your Majesty. So do—'' Appalled,

she bit her tongue at the inappropriately personal remark.

His lips curved in a hint of a smile. "Damn. Don't tell me it's improper to compliment the king?"

Erin wondered if her entire body was blushing. His expression made her feel as if he were hungry and she was the first course. "Of course not, sir, but I am in your service."

He nodded. "So what's the proper way to compliment a king?"

Erin took a careful breath and tried to unscramble her brain. "If I may say so, Your Majesty looks quite dashing this evening."

"Dashing," he said. "Sounds like something out of an old English novel. I guess that means it wouldn't be proper to say you look hot enough to start another three-alarm fire in downtown Chicago?"

The same was true of him, she thought. "That's correct, sir," she said.

"But you won't mind if I give the fire department a call to warn them about you," he said, his mouth unsmiling, but his eyes full of masculine humor.

"Me?"

His gaze fell over her with dangerous awareness. "Yes, you."

Three

Daniel led Erin through the grand lobby of the hotel where the ball was being held. Sweeping her into a brass-lined elevator, he tugged at his collar as soon as the doors closed. "We won't stay long. I've grown impatient with these affairs during the last couple of years. I'd rather do almost anything than just make an appearance."

"Pardon me, sir, but you know that your appearance at state and social functions will be quite important to the people of Altaria," Erin pointed out.

He nodded. "I know. I can dress to suit the occasion. But I also know that the personality and vision of the man wearing the crown determines his role. I plan to spend as much time doing things as I will spend making appearances."

Erin felt a ripple of uneasiness as she thought of her father's diametrically opposed view of Daniel's role as king. She looked at the strong, dynamic man in front of her and wondered how she would be able to convince him that he would be more of a figurehead. Not bloody likely. Especially when her own opinion was beginning to waver. She felt a lightning-fast jab of pain and slammed the door on her thoughts. She had a job to do for her country, for her father.

Daniel led her away from the main entrance to the ballroom down the hall and to another door. "We decided it would call less attention to me if I weren't announced," he said. "The press will have to search for me."

Erin glanced at him and couldn't help shaking her head at his comment.

He stopped. "What?"

"Nothing, sir," she said.

Daniel sighed. "I really don't want to have to do this, but—"

Erin cringed. She suspected she knew what was coming.

"I order you to tell me what you're thinking," he said. "For the rest of the evening."

Erin gaped at him in shock. "The entire evening, sir?" she echoed, aghast.

He nodded. "So cough it up. Why did you shake your head when I said the press would have to search for me?"

Erin closed her eyes in embarrassment. "Must I, sir?"

"Yes."

She swallowed a howl of frustration. "If you want to avoid attention, sir, you need to shrink your height and intelligence. And you would have to do something to make yourself look more plain. You draw attention just by entering the room."

He dipped his head close to hers. "You're a lot more fun when you're honest," he murmured and took her hand. "Let's go."

He pulled her into a huge room filled with beautifully dressed party-goers. Music emanated from an orchestra playing on the far end. The marble-floored ballroom was decorated with mirrors and crystal chandeliers. Tables of appetizers and pastries lined one corner of the room while waiters carried trays of champagne throughout the crowd.

Erin remembered when she had accompanied her father to other parties. Her job had been essentially to disappear once the announcements had been made. "I can excuse myself while you make your necessary rounds, sir," she offered, disengaging her hand from his.

He frowned at her. "Why?"

"Because I'm certain there are people with whom you must speak, sir."

"Is there a reason you can't speak to them too?"

Confused, she slowly shook her head. "No, sir. I thought my purpose for the evening was to provide the appearance of an escort and stay in the background as much as possible.''

"No," he said. "Your job for the evening is to make this bearable, and you can start by ditching the 'sir.' If anyone overhears you, it will make them curious. You probably need to pretend to like me.''

Her stomach twisted, and, at a loss, she nervously twined her fingers together. "If I may ask, si—'' She broke off. "How am I to make this bearable? And how should I pretend to like you?'' she asked, determined to keep the panic from her voice.

He shrugged. "Damned if I know. Here comes my brother Brett. You can practice with him.''

Brett patted his shoulder. "Good of you to show up, YM,'' Brett said, abbreviating the royal address.

"How are you keeping the press at bay?'' Daniel asked, surveying the room.

"There are a few here, but they're wearing special name tags and red roses. Who can resist a rose?''

"Clever,'' Daniel said, admiring his brother's savvy. "I'd like you to meet Erin Lawrence. Erin, this is my brother Brett. He's the master of public relations for Connelly Corporation and the reason I'm here tonight.''

Daniel watched his lady-killer brother give Erin a glance of approval and felt a swift jab of protectiveness toward her.

Brett took Erin's hand and lifted it to his lips. *"Enchanté mademoiselle.''*

"Merci beaucoup, Your Hi—'' Her eyes widened

in alarm as she looked at Daniel. "I'm sorry, si—"
She shook her head. "I'm sorry. It slipped."

"Years of breeding," Daniel said dryly.

"I don't mind being called Your Highness," Brett
said smoothly. "Particularly by such a lovely young
woman."

Daniel fought a ripple of irritation. "Excuse us
just a moment," he said to Erin, then moved a few
steps away with his brother. "Stop hitting on her.
She's young."

"Not that young," Brett said. "Her accent is sexy
and that body—"

"She's only twenty-two, and she's spent her life
in boarding schools. She might as well have been
raised in a convent."

Brett lifted a dark brow. "Who are you trying to
convince? Me or you?"

Me, Daniel thought. The last thing in the world
he needed right now was to be sexually distracted
by his prim and proper protocol instructor, but
damned if he wasn't. "How's Mom?" he asked,
knowing his mother was still struggling with the
double loss of her father and brother.

Brett's face grew serious. "Perfectly composed.
Just don't look at her eyes very long or your gut
will start to ache for her."

Daniel quickly glanced around the room and spotted his parents. "Dad's sticking by her side."

"Like glue," Brett said.

"That will help," Daniel said.

"Knowing that you're accepting the title and the job that goes with it helps too," Brett added quietly.

Daniel felt a gnawing impatience to get on with his transition, but he knew change took time. "Go make your rounds," he said.

"Thanks for coming. I know it's a strange time for you. If you're smart, though, you could take a little solace from Erin Lawrence."

"There'll be a heat wave in Chicago in January before I take romantic advice from you."

"She looks pretty hot to me," Brett shot back, then scooted through the crowd to avoid Daniel's wrath.

Sighing, Daniel returned to Erin. "I see my parents. Let's go say hello."

Erin lifted her hand to her throat. "Your mother? The princess?"

"My mother, Emma Rosemere Connelly," he said, although he was accustomed to the star-struck response. Emma inspired admiration of mythic proportions. "Remember to ditch the titles," he said, guiding her through the crowd.

His mother was dressed in a black gown. Most would admire her sophisticated beauty and miss the grief, but Daniel immediately caught the sadness in his mother's gaze and felt a twist inside him. He kissed her cheek. "You look beautiful."

Emma smiled. "I'm going to miss you," she said, and turned her gaze on Erin. "Ah, you must be the woman with the formidable job of teaching my son royal protocol. Erin Lawrence. A pleasure to meet you.''

Daniel felt Erin start to dip into a curtsey and slipped his arm around her waist to prevent it. She shot him a look of dark chagrin.

"It's my honor to meet you, Your Hi—'' She broke off and smiled. "Mrs. Connelly. At the boarding school I attended, you're greatly revered.''

"Not always," Emma said with a smile of reminiscence. "Years ago, the teachers despaired over my lack of interest in those tiresome etiquette classes. It's amazing what time and distance can do. Please meet my husband, Grant.''

Daniel's father greeted Erin and shook his head. "You're so young for such a challenging job," he said, glancing pointedly at Daniel.

"I was just thinking the same thing," Emma said. "It can be lonely in a different country. You must join us for dinner. I'll call Daniel soon to arrange a time.''

"Thank you," Erin said, appearing stunned as Daniel led her away.

He snagged two glasses of champagne and lifted one glass to Erin's lips. "Drink up. Having a father as foreign minister, you must have met plenty of renowned people before.''

She took a quick sip, then another. "I have," she admitted. "But your family is so kind. Your mother, your father, your brother, they obviously care for you so much and it's clearly reciprocal. How can you bear to leave them for Altaria?"

Daniel glanced away. She'd unknowingly touched a tender spot he kept concealed. So far, the most difficult part of accepting the throne would be moving far from the people he trusted most to a place where he wasn't sure there would be anyone he could trust. He met her gaze. "I guess a big part of the reason I choose to leave is to honor my family's bond. Nothing will change it, titles, oceans, nothing."

Erin's eyes grew shiny, and she glanced at the floor. He wondered what was racing through her mind.

"Say it aloud," he said.

She looked up at him in surprise. "Pardon?"

"Say what you're thinking."

"I'm trying to imagine what it would be like to have a family like yours, to share that kind of love."

"Don't you have that with your father?"

He looked into her eyes and in one swift moment, he saw a mile-wide streak of loneliness that shook him. As if she were afraid he'd seen too much, she looked away. "Of course," she murmured, but the words were spoken too late with too little conviction.

Daniel would have to think about that later, he decided. When he wasn't thinking about the three hundred other items on his to-do list. He downed the rest of his champagne and glanced at her averted head. "You're falling down on your job," he said.

Her head immediately shot up. "Pardon?"

"You're supposed to make this ball bearable."

"I hadn't quite figured out how to do that," she said and took another sip of her champagne. "What do you usually enjoy doing at these affairs?"

"Figuring out how to leave early," he said. "What do you usually enjoy doing at these affairs?"

Her lips twitched. "I make a game of guessing what's in the appetizers, and sometimes I waltz."

"Let's head for the food," he said, guiding her toward the tables laden with food. "I'm not big on waltzing."

"You must waltz," she said firmly. "You will be expected to lead the first dance for many occasions."

"I'll appoint an official waltzing representative," he joked, and chuckled at the look of disapproval she shot him.

They drew near the tables, and Daniel chose an appetizer. He lifted the small bite to his mouth, but Erin stopped him halfway.

"The game is to guess the appetizer *before* you eat it," she said.

"I thought I was supposed to guess after I ate it."

"That wouldn't present as much of a challenge," she said. "Unless the food is very bad." She eyed the small morsel of food. "I guess that's crab and mushroom."

"I agree," he said.

She looked at him and groaned. "You are supposed to guess something different."

"You stole the best guess," he said with a shrug.

"I didn't steal anything," she protested.

"Let's see if you're right." Daniel lifted the appetizer to her mouth.

Her eyes widened in surprise, but she opened her mouth. Daniel watched her tongue curl around the bite of food and felt an unsettling twist of arousal. Her attempted perfection goaded the hell out of him. She made him want to tease her. He wanted to pull down her hair, make her laugh and mess up her lipstick by kissing the breath and starch out of her.

He had to keep telling himself she was only twenty-two, twelve years younger than he.

She swallowed and licked her lips, and Daniel felt another twist of arousal. The sight of her pink tongue generated a dozen forbidden images in his mind.

"Definitely crab and mushroom," she said. "I choose the next one." She glanced over the table and pointed to a dessert tray. "Your turn to guess."

"That's easy. It's a puff pastry," Daniel said.

"But anything could be inside," she said. "What's inside?"

Daniel lifted one of the pastries and scrutinized it. "These remind me of you. Easy to see what you are on the outside, but I can't help wondering what's inside," he said, searching her eyes. At times, she reminded him of a lost little girl. Other times, he wanted to strip off her clothes and know her every way a man could know a woman.

She looked away as if she didn't want him to see too much. "I'm not that complicated," she murmured, then glanced back up at him. "Are you stalling with your guess?"

"Butterscotch swirl," he said and lifted the pastry to her lips. He didn't have time to be curious about this woman, but he was.

She opened her mouth and accepted the small bite of dessert. "How did you know it was butterscotch?"

"Insider information. Butterscotch is my father's favorite. The menu planners try to please him when they know he'll be attending."

"What is your favorite?"

"Variety," Daniel said as he caught sight of a press representative. "I see someone with a rose. Let's head for that alcove."

Daniel led her into a small, dim room and closed the doors behind them. The outer wall was lined with windows that allowed the city lights to shine into the room, and the orchestral music was piped in from a speaker in the ceiling.

Aside from the music, the only sound Erin could hear was her pounding heart. She was alone with Daniel Connelly. She'd been alone with him before, but the thick veil of formality had always provided her with protection and comfort. Tonight Daniel had insisted on dropping the formality, and he had treated her more like a date than an employee. More like a woman than a protocol teacher.

She'd watched the tenderness he'd extended to his mother and couldn't help but feel moved. She'd seen the combination of camaraderie and mutual respect he shared with his brother and felt acutely the lack of the family she'd always wanted, but never had.

She was supposed to discourage Daniel from taking the throne because he was wrong for Altaria, but the more she learned about Daniel, the more confused she became. Heaven help her, she felt his eyes on her and could hardly breathe.

She heard the first strains of a familiar waltz and an idea hit her. Desperate for a diversion from her thoughts, she grasped at it. "This is a waltz," she said. "I can teach you how. You'll need to know how once you move into the palace." Biting her lip, she lifted her arms into dance position.

"You're going to teach me?" he echoed, taking her hand and curling his other hand around her waist.

His closeness halted her breath all over again and second thoughts slammed through her. She cleared her throat and trained her eyes on his left shoulder. "Yes, the waltz is done in steps of three. One-two-three, one-two-three." After years of training, her feet moved automatically. Thank goodness. She continued counting and he slowly followed. Before she knew it, however, he was leading her.

Erin looked at him suspiciously. "I thought you said you didn't waltz."

"I said I'm not big on waltzing," he said. "Do you really think Emma Rosemere Connelly would allow her firstborn son to take a pass on social dance lessons even if he'd rather be playing football?"

An image played across her mind of Daniel at a younger age futilely protesting dance lessons. She smiled. "I suppose not. But you actually waltz quite well for someone who dislikes it."

The music slowed, and so did Daniel. The blatant male sexuality in his expression made her heart race. He lowered his forehead to hers and whispered, "Maybe I needed a different dance partner."

Four

"I know there's more work to be done during this transition, and I'm ready to get on with it," Daniel told his brother Brett three days later as he made another note on a new marketing proposal for Connelly Corporation.

"What do you mean?" Brett asked.

Unable to sit, Daniel stood as he struggled with a nagging impatience that was becoming all too familiar. He was tired of feeling split between two worlds. "I mean the facade is wearing thin. If I were doing this my way, then I would be in Altaria now. I'm still not getting the information I want from Erin's father, the foreign minister, as fast as I want it. It's almost as if everyone's throwing logs on the road in front of me to slow me down."

Brett threw him a cautious glance. "You know you're not going to be able to change everything in a day."

"I know," Daniel said. "But until I get all the information I want, I can't do anything. I'm letting you know because I'm cutting back on Connelly time. I'll tell my assistant sometime during the next week."

Brett nodded his head slowly. "You know your succession to the throne will hit the news right away."

Daniel took a deep breath. He knew his life would be turned upside down once the media found out he was accepting the throne. "It's going to be part of the job. Just like all this royal protocol Miss Perfect Erin is trying to teach me."

Daniel glanced up at that moment to catch Miss Perfect right behind his brother. He saw the look of hurt on her face and swallowed an oath. He shouldn't take his frustration out on her, but damn if the woman hadn't said Your Majesty and sir to him so many times since the ball he thought he could break a window.

"Let's finish this later," Daniel said to Brett.

Confusion crossed Brett's face. "But—"

"Hello, Erin," Daniel said meaningfully and watched realization cross his brother's face.

"Oh." Brett nodded. "Later. Keep me posted. Hi, Erin," he said as he strode out the door.

"Your Highness," she murmured to his back.

"Your Majesty," she then said to Daniel in a voice that dripped ice. "Begging your pardon. Perhaps you forgot that we were to meet for an hour just before lunch."

"I did forget," he admitted and closed the door behind her. "And I offended you. I'm sorry."

She waved her hand. "Oh, no, sir. It's my job to present the best possible example to you, and you are certainly more than entitled to your opinion. It's unfortunate that I've been unsuccessful in conveying to you the importance of tradition and royal protocol in your new role as King of Altaria."

Erin's clipped voice cut his conscience like knives. Why did he feel as if he'd just kicked a puppy? He rubbed his face. "You're right. I don't put the same priority on tradition as you do. But just because I don't buy everything you tell me doesn't give me the right to hurt your feelings."

Her eyes widened. "No, sir. You didn't hurt my feel—"

"I damn well did," he said, cutting her off. "And I don't like that I did it. We need a truce."

"A truce, sir?" she echoed doubtfully.

"We're not going to get anywhere if you stick to your guns and I stick to mine. I'll work on understanding why this royal protocol is so important if you'll work on figuring out how to bring part of my world to Altaria."

Her eyebrows furrowed in confusion. "I'm not certain what you mean, sir."

Daniel tossed his pen on his desk in frustration. "I mean we're going to take turns. I'm going to try to look at things from your point of view and you're going to look at things from my point of view."

Erin frowned. "But how can we accomplish that, sir? I know very little of your life."

Daniel wondered if part of the reason it drove him nuts for Erin to call him sir was because it reminded him of their twelve-year age difference. "You're going to have to spend some extra time with me, and the first new rule is no more 'Your Majesty' or 'sir' unless we're specifically discussing royal protocol."

She lifted her chin. "Begging your pardon, sir, it is entirely correct for me to address you as Your Majesty."

"It may be correct, but it bugs the hell out of me."

"Begging your pardon again, sir, but you must know that everyone in Altaria will address you in this manner."

"Unless I request them to address me differently. Correct?"

Reluctance shimmered in her eyes. "Yes, sir."

"Drop the sir," he told her. "If you need to fill in the gap, say my name. Daniel."

"Yes-s-s—" She drew out the word as if adding sir was compulsory. She glared at him. "Yes, Daniel."

"Thank you, Erin. Tomorrow's Saturday. I'll pick you up around 11:00 a.m. Wear jeans."

Erin blinked. "I don't have any jeans. The schools I attended didn't allow them and my father doesn't approve of them."

"Well, you've graduated from boarding school and Daddy's not here," Daniel said, struggling to keep the edge from his voice. He had more than one reason to be irritated with Erin's father. "You need casual clothes to blend in where we're going, and the closest to casual I've seen you wear was my sweat pants. Buy a couple of pairs of jeans and whatever else you need and put them on the Connelly account."

She gave a slow, reluctant nod of agreement. "When will we have our next royal protocol consultation?" she asked, determination in her voice.

"After our outing tomorrow," he said and figured they were even. Erin would probably dislike their field trip as much as he detested the protocol lessons.

The following morning Daniel pulled his sport utility vehicle up in front of Erin's hotel and opened his car door only to spot her striding through the revolving door to meet him. She wore jeans, a cuddly sweater and a casual overcoat, and her hair hung in a shiny curtain to her shoulders.

"Good morning, Daniel," she said, meeting his gaze so directly he felt as if he'd been broadsided.

"Good morning, Erin." His attention caught by her hair, he helped her into the car and got in. "You look good,'' he said as he pulled the car out into traffic.

She lifted an eyebrow in disbelief. ''My father would probably disown me.''

''Is your dad that uptight, or is he afraid he's going to have to beat the men off you?''

Erin did a double take. ''Beat the men off me?'' she said in disbelief.

''Yeah. If you wear your hair down like that all the time and bag the perfection syndrome, you'll have to fight them off.''

Erin turned silent. ''That problem hasn't presented itself so far. Besides, my father is well aware of the fact that I'm not perfect. You've said your family is competitive. You should understand the drive for perfection.''

''My father always taught us there's a difference between striving for perfection and doing your best. Doing your best means you recognize you can make a contribution by pushing yourself to be the best you can be. Striving for perfection just makes you cranky.''

Erin looked at Daniel and swallowed a sigh. She so wanted not to like him. Disliking Daniel would make her job so much easier. When he spouted something about perfection that went against everything her father had taught her, yet somehow resonated in her heart, she was at a loss to maintain her disapproval of him. ''You're very fortunate to have grown up with such supportive parents.''

"You've said that more than once. What's your mother like?"

Erin laced her fingers together. "She died when I was very young. My father's professional position was demanding, so I've spent most of my life in boarding schools."

Daniel was silent for a long moment. "That must have been tough."

Erin felt her heart tighten. She didn't want him to feel sorry for her. "I was actually quite fortunate. I've been given the best possible education."

Daniel nodded, but he didn't look convinced. He pulled into an alley behind an older building and stopped the car.

"Where are—"

He took her hands and looked into her eyes, causing her words to stall. "Just because you didn't get the same kind of support I got growing up doesn't mean you didn't deserve it."

Her heart squeezed tight again at his combination of strength and gentleness. It was almost as if he'd known the words she'd longed to hear. But he couldn't possibly, she told herself. He couldn't possibly.

"Yo! Daniel!" a man called outside the car, interrupting the moment that seemed to move her ever closer to Daniel. "Open the trunk."

Erin looked at Daniel in confusion. "The trunk. What are we doing?"

"We're at a soup kitchen that operates out of the

basement of a church. I get donations from some of the local restaurants, pick up sandwiches on Saturday morning, and we feed some people who need a meal.''

Astonished, Erin stared at the men unloading the back of Daniel's vehicle. "You do this every Saturday?"

"For the past four years," he said, exiting his side of the car and coming around to open her door. He offered his hand to assist her. "You look surprised."

Erin accepted his hand to make the big step to the ground. "I don't know what I expected, but I didn't expect this," she said, as their eyes met.

He skimmed his fingers down a strand of her hair. "I'm a hands-on kind of man."

Erin felt a dip in her stomach. Her father would be less than thrilled with that information. She pulled her hand from his. "How can I help?"

"You can watch. You don't have to do anything," he told her, striding past her to pick up a huge tray of sandwiches.

Erin hurried after him. "But I'd like to help," she said.

He met her gaze and assessed her. "Okay, but you need to understand you'll see all kinds of people in there today. College graduates, homeless families and a few alcoholics, but no royal titles."

Slightly affronted by his tone, she frowned. "I'm not a snob."

He lifted a dark eyebrow. "Could've fooled me."

"I may be a bit strict about the rules of protocol, but I'm not a snob," she insisted.

He nodded, although he didn't appear entirely convinced. "Okay. If you want to help, I'll introduce you to the soup kitchen leader. Joe!" he called as he walked through the open entrance into a large room filled with tables covered with white paper.

Erin followed Daniel and couldn't help noticing the way his jeans molded to his long legs and muscular backside. She blinked at her observation. Heaven help her. She was ogling His Majesty. Again. Her cheeks burned with a mixture of consternation and self-consciousness.

A tall man with a scrubby beard and friendly eyes approached them. He thumped Daniel on the back. "Good to see you."

"Same," Daniel said and cocked his head toward Erin as he set the huge sandwich tray down on a long serving table. "I brought a visitor with me this time. Joe Graham, meet Erin Lawrence. She wants you to put her to work."

"It's a pleasure to meet you, Mr. Graham," Erin said.

Joe beamed. "My pleasure. Call me Joe. Love the accent and so will the masses. You don't have to serve. I just want you to talk for the next two hours."

Daniel groaned.

"Pardon?" Erin said, confused.

Daniel returned to her side. "Joe likes your accent. American men in general like your accent. It's sexy.''

Astonished, Erin gasped and shook her head. She swallowed her amazement. "There is nothing sexy about my accent," she said, and lowered her voice. "There's nothing sexy about me,''she said more to herself than to him. She should never forget that Daniel was light-years ahead of her in sexual experience.

Daniel's gaze was so intense he could have leveled a forest with it. "Who told you that?"

Erin got an odd jumpy feeling in her stomach. "Well, no one. But no one has told me differently either."

"Hm," he said, and the sound was short, but left her filled with a hundred questions.

She never got the answers, as she was put to work ladling soup into disposable bowls, while others set out plates with sandwiches and cups of hot coffee. Daniel had been correct about the wide range of people who came for food. In her conversations with them, she observed that they represented all demographics and all walks of life. She enjoyed chatting with the people and couldn't remember a time she'd felt so useful and appreciated.

Just as the line began to wind down, Joe let out a whoop of happiness. "TV camera crews are coming down the steps. Everybody give me a big smile and think *donations*.''

In no time, Daniel appeared by her side. "We

can't stay. I don't want to be recognized, and I don't want them going after you,'' he murmured into her ear. The door where they'd entered was blocked by a group of people waiting to sit down. Daniel closed his hand around her arm. ''Follow me,'' he said, guiding her down a short hallway with three doors. He tried the first two doors, but they were locked. He finally found one that opened.

''Bingo,'' he said and scowled when he looked inside. ''It'll have to do. We shouldn't have to wait long.''

''Wait where?'' Erin asked, not liking the expression she saw on his face.

''In this closet.''

Five

―――

"**W**hy on earth would we need to go into a closet?" Erin demanded.

"Hey, Daniel," a voice called from the main serving area. "Where's Daniel?"

"That's why," Daniel said, ushering her into the closet and closing the door. It was as black as pitch. More calls for Daniel echoed down the hall.

Erin felt Daniel's arm slide behind her waist and his hand gently covered her mouth. "Be quiet for the next few minutes," he whispered.

He touched her as if he'd known she might be uneasy in the dark with him, and she felt another stone fall from her defenses. She stood in silence and breathed in his scent and absorbed his strength.

He stood close enough for her to feel his chest brush hers. She could barely hear the sound of footsteps above her pounding heart.

She felt safe and breathless at the same time.

"I think they're gone, but we probably need to wait a few minutes before they leave the building," he finally said in a low voice after a door down the hall closed. "You okay?"

She nodded. "Yes," she whispered, reluctant to break the odd spell.

"After I dragged you in here, it occurred to me that you might have a fear of enclosed spaces. But it was too late."

The sound of his voice was low and intimate, the same voice he might use in bed with a lover. The knowledge warmed her from the inside out. She took a careful half breath. "Even as a child, I always liked small places," she confessed. "Something about them made me feel safer."

She felt his fingers sift through her hair. "Sometimes when I look at you, I wonder what you were like as a little girl."

Her stomach twisted at his remark. Although her childhood hadn't been miserable, she'd always wanted to belong, to be needed. She felt a strange knot of emotion form in her throat.

"Were you always so determined to be perfect?" he asked.

The darkness made it easier to talk. "I tried, but of course, I never was. I always thought that if I were perfect then someone would—'' Her throat swelled shut around the words.

''Someone would what?'' he prompted.

''Someone would want me with them all the time, and I wouldn't have to be alone,'' she said, and felt a tear burn a trail down her cheek. Shocked at the display of emotion, she blinked and thanked her lucky stars that Daniel couldn't see her. She tried to step back, but he tightened his hold on her.

He lifted his hand to her hair again, and she held her breath, terrified he would find her damp cheek. She was fully dressed, but she had never felt more naked. His hand grazed her cheek and abruptly stopped.

She heard and felt his sharp intake of breath. He lowered his fingers to her lips and chin and his mouth touched hers. It was a tender caress, reassuring and searching. She felt him wind his fingers through the back of her hair, tilting her mouth for better access. Everything about the way he kissed her told her she needn't be lonely. At least at this very moment, it was okay not to be perfect.

He brushed his lips back and forth against hers, and the very air in the closet seemed to change. His tongue swept over hers, making her heart jump. He made a low sound of approval and shifted slightly, urging her into the cradle of his hard thighs. His tongue dallied seductively with hers, making her warm.

She instinctively lifted her arms around his neck

and the position brought her breasts against his hard chest. He slid his hands just beneath her sweater. She felt the warmth of his fingers on the skin above her jeans and her breath hitched in her throat.

"What fool ever told you that you weren't perfect?" he muttered against her lips. He took her mouth with an edgy hunger that was echoed in the sensual thrust of his lower body against hers.

Light-headed, she drew back and gasped for air. She took several breaths before oxygen hit her brain and she realized she was kissing His Majesty. Panic rushed through her, and she felt the awful urge to hiccup. Erin covered her face and took a deep breath. "Oh, Lord, what am I doing?" she whispered to herself.

"Whatever it is, you're doing it damn well," he said.

Taking another breath, Erin bit her lip and thanked heaven for the darkness because she was certain she was a neon shade of red from head to toe. She cleared her throat and stepped backward, as much as she could in the tight closet, immediately struggling with a sense of loss. "Um, do you think we could maybe forget what we just did?"

Silence followed.

"No," Daniel finally said, and the single syllable oozed sexual suggestion.

Erin swallowed a groan. "Do you think we could pretend to forget?"

He leaned closer and she felt his fingers whisk through her hair like a ghost's touch. "No."

An anxious knot formed in her chest. "Then what are we going to do? I just kissed the incoming King of Altaria," she said, unable to keep her dismay from her voice.

"That's one way of looking at it," he said in a voice that managed to be both calm and sexy.

"And what's another way?" she asked.

"You kissed me—Daniel. And I kissed you," he said. "Next time it won't be in the dark."

After he and Erin successfully escaped the notice of the local TV news team and returned to his condo, Daniel dutifully held up his end of the bargain and endured his protocol lesson.

It was tough because he was distracted as hell by her mouth. Every time she spoke, he thought about how she had tasted and felt. Every time she moved her mouth, he thought about all the things he wanted to do to her.

He met her eyes and found her staring at him impatiently. "Do I need to repeat myself, sir?"

God forbid, Daniel thought and shook his head. "You said that I'm supposed to allow others to formally announce me before I approach people. In general, Altarian citizens will bow or curtsey, address me first as Your Majesty, then use sir. My question is, how much of a snit am I supposed to get into if someone forgets to bow?"

Erin blinked. "That's entirely your prerogative, sir, but if you'd like to use King Thomas as an example, he simply ignored those who didn't show him proper courtesy or respect."

"So I'm not expected to put them on the rack or throw them off the island if they don't curtsey correctly," he said.

Her lips twitched at his exaggeration. "That would be correct, sir."

"I suppose I could require any curtsey transgressors to give Jordan here a bath," Daniel said, nodding toward the dog snoring in front of the fire.

She looked at him in disbelief. "You're planning to bring your dog to the palace with you, sir?"

"Sure am," he said. "I can't bring my family and I have this funny premonition that I'm not going to have a lot of friends when I first arrive." He paused, watching her facial expressions shift. "From your surprise, I'll guess that King Thomas didn't have a dog."

"Correct, sir," she said, casting a doubtful glance at the dog.

"You look as though you're trying to figure out how to teach Jordan royal protocol," he said, and walked closer to her. "Don't underestimate him. He might be easier to train than me."

She pressed her lips together as if she didn't dare say what she was thinking.

"Say it aloud," he said.

"I suspect Jordan might very well be easier to

train as long as I kept an ample supply of pizza available, sir."

"I need more than pizza," Daniel said, wondering how she would look naked on his bed.

Erin looked away. "I'm sure you do, sir."

Daniel stifled a sigh at her 'sir'. "I bet you're more of a cat person," he said.

"I actually always wanted a dog, sir, but the boarding schools didn't allow pets other than gold-fish, and my father was too busy to care for a pet."

"Let me guess," Daniel said, teasing her out of her oh-so-proper mode. "A poodle."

She lifted her chin. "They are very intelligent, sir."

Daniel grinned. "And prissy."

"They don't shed or slobber," she returned and quickly added, "sir."

Daniel couldn't forget how her body had felt in his arms. "If you weren't so young, I'd kiss you again," he told her.

"I'm not too young," she retorted, then chagrin crossed her face. "But your instincts are entirely correct that kissing me would be inappropriate, sir."

"Why?"

"Because I am in your service, sir," she said.

"What if I fired you?"

Her eyes rounded. "You can't! You must not, sir. I mean—" She broke off as if she couldn't find the words.

Daniel dipped his head to catch her eyes. "Are you not attracted to me?"

She glanced at him, then away. "I didn't say that, sir."

"Then you *are* attracted to me."

She bit her lip. "I didn't say that either, but—"

"Then which is it?"

Erin gave a heavy sigh. "I'm sure I don't have to tell you that you're very attractive, sir."

That wasn't enough for Daniel. "But how do I affect you?"

Erin frowned at him. "It's not appropriate for you to affect me."

"The same way it wasn't appropriate for you to want a poodle? It didn't change the fact that you wanted one, did it?"

Her eyes were dark and full of forbidden secrets. "There is a very big difference between a poodle and you," she said.

He lifted a strand of her hair. "I can't disagree," he said and tugged her closer. He lowered his mouth a breath from hers. "I won't order you to kiss me. I won't use my position that way," he said.

Erin closed her eyes, lost in a swirl of contradicting emotions. "I shouldn't kiss you," she said desperately. "It's not right." Not right for many reasons, she thought, feeling as if she were twisting in the wind. She was supposed to have a professional relationship with Daniel. Plus there was the matter of her father. Kissing Daniel, even liking him, made her feel disloyal.

But her father didn't know him, she argued with herself. If her father knew Daniel, he would... Her stomach tightened with dread. If her father knew Daniel, he still wouldn't like him. Her father wanted a king who wouldn't upset the apple cart. Her father wanted a king he could keep under his thumb, and His Majesty or not, Daniel would never be kept under any man's thumb.

Frustration crowded her chest. She wondered if she could learn the same lesson of independence. She slowly opened her eyes and stared into his. So strong, so bold. He made her question everything that had come before him. He made her want to be as strong as he was. How in the world could she refuse him?

How could she not?

"It's time for me to go, sir," she finally managed, feeling his eyes burn through her.

Erin returned to her too-quiet hotel room and decided to go to bed early. Steeped in questions about her father, Daniel and herself, she pulled the covers over her head. The phone startled her. She glanced at the clock and knew it was her father calling. He would ask how she was progressing. He would ask if she had discouraged Daniel or reined him in. Not bloody likely.

The phone continued to ring, and she held her

breath. How could she help her father to see that Daniel was a man of honor and that he would genuinely care for the people of Altaria? How could she convince him that Daniel could bring a new combination of strength and compassion to the throne?

The phone stopped ringing, and Erin covered her face. She was bloody well in a pit of trouble. Convincing her father would be difficult enough. How could she convince Daniel that they shouldn't get involved when she was having trouble convincing herself?

Daniel insisted that Erin join him on Monday so she could gain a picture of the work environment he would be leaving. Erin took a cab to the Connelly corporate offices. She stared up at the modern glass-and-steel structure, reminded again of the Connelly family's wealth and success. Entering the mahogany-paneled reception area, she lingered over the pictures of the various Connelly family members who had created and built the company over the years. The more time she spent with Daniel, the more curious she grew about his father's side of his family.

Security allowed her to pass and she took the elevator to the floor that housed Daniel's office. Behind the receptionist's desk, she saw a beautiful watercolor of one of Altaria's beaches. Giving her name to the receptionist, she stared at the painting and tried to imagine Daniel in the setting. It wasn't difficult imagining him on the beach. In the palace, though, was a different matter.

Daniel rounded the corner wearing a dark wool suit that emphasized his broad shoulders and height. He waved her toward him. "Come on back. I'll show you my office, then I'm making an announcement."

She was amazed at how easily he shifted from casual sportsman to sophisticated businessman. Perhaps that was why he wasn't overly concerned about sliding into his new role as ruler. As she passed through a hall of offices and cubicles, she suspected he'd sharpened his leadership skills at Connelly Corporation.

"Is this entire floor devoted to marketing?"

"Actually two floors, and this is just corporate headquarters," he said. "We have marketing offices all over the world." He guided her past a young woman with honey-colored hair and blue-green eyes. "Erin Lawrence, this is Kimberly Lindgren, my assistant. Smart as a whip and quick."

Kimberly shot Daniel a fond, but skeptical glance. "Such flattery. Are you softening the blow that I'll have to work overtime tonight?"

Daniel chuckled. "Not this time."

"It's a pleasure to meet you," Erin said, admiring the woman's confidence and ease with Daniel.

"The pleasure's mine. Lovely accent," Kimberly said.

"Thank you," Erin said and followed Daniel into

his large, lush corner office. The view from his full-length glass windows took her breath. "It's beautiful," she said. "What a pleasure to work in these surroundings every day."

He came to the window just behind her. "Lake Michigan," he said. "I've always been partial to a great view." Glancing down at her, he stroked his finger under her chin and met her eyes. "Here's another great view," he murmured, clearly meaning her.

Erin's stomach dipped. She shouldn't care if he found her attractive, she told herself. But she did. Confused by her conflicting emotions, she laced her fingers together and looked out the window again. "It must be terribly difficult for you to give all of this up for Altaria, even to be king. Your family, your country and all of this," she said, waving her hand.

"Well, the Connellys might have a large slice of the pie, but we don't own all of Lake Michigan," he said lightly.

"Still, I wonder how you can give up all that is familiar to you for Altaria. Here, you're surrounded by supportive family, employees and friends. It will be very different in Altaria," she said, her father's hostility weighing heavy on her mind.

"I know I'm not entering a friendly situation. It won't be the first time I've had to win over the opposition. But I can make a difference in Altaria," he said with quiet but rock-solid confidence.

Something in his voice made her believe him.

"The end of my Connelly Corporation days is right around the corner," he said and glanced toward his doorway. "Which is why I'm taking Kimberly into my confidence today."

"Are you sure that's wise? I thought you didn't want to make an announcement yet," Erin said.

"I'm not making an announcement, but it's fair to let my closest employee know my plans. She won't have to keep the secret long." He punched the intercom button on his phone. "Kimberly, could you come into my office for a minute please?"

"Yes, Daniel," the woman said.

Erin bit her lip at the woman's familiarity. "Are all Americans as casual with their bosses?"

"I prefer it," Daniel said, then did a double take. "Are you jealous?" he asked in a low voice.

Erin felt her temperature climb ten degrees. "Absolutely not. I'm simply unaccustomed to the casual way employees address their superiors here."

"Kimberly's very attractive and intelligent, but I don't make a habit of getting romantically involved with my assistants," Daniel said as if Erin hadn't denied his accusation.

"The same way you've avoided romantic involvement with me," she said. Immediately appalled at her lack of propriety, she blurted, "Oh, my God, I can't believe I said that."

Daniel shot her a dangerous grin and moved toward her. "The thing you need to understand, Erin, is that you're different."

How? she wanted to ask, but managed to keep her mouth shut.

Daniel continued, "And we're not nearly as involved as I'd like to be."

Erin gulped at the way he made her knees dip.

"Daniel?" Kimberly said from the doorway. She glanced curiously from her boss to Erin.

Erin locked her knees and resisted the urge to fan her cheeks.

"Please close the door behind you," he said and leaned against his desk. "Have a seat."

Kimberly sat down and waited.

"This is strictly confidential, but I wanted you to know because there will be a period of transition during which you must limit your vacation days. I'm leaving Connelly Corporation in a couple of weeks," he said.

Kimberly's eyes widened. "Leaving? But you're a Connelly. What will you do?" she asked, shaking her head. "And I can't imagine who can replace you."

"My brother Justin," Daniel said.

Kimberly lowered her head. "Justin," she echoed. "He's so..." She appeared to search for the right words. "So...serious," she finally said.

"Exactly," Daniel agreed. "He'll work himself into an early grave if left to his own devices. I'd like you to make sure he chills out every now and then."

Kimberly blinked. "How?"

"I don't know. It'll take some creativity," he muttered.

Kimberly looked totally confused. "I don't know what to say. You've been a terrific boss. I've learned so much from you. May I ask why you're leaving?"

"I'm moving to Altaria," he said. "With the death of my grandfather and uncle, the throne goes to the eldest Altarian male."

It took a moment for his news to digest. She stood and lifted her hand to her open mouth. "Oh my goodness, you're going to be king!" She shook her head again. "King of Altaria. It's a small island, isn't it? Well, I suppose it's not that different than being a head honcho at Connelly Corporation. I don't know what to say." She looked at Erin. "You must be involved in some way," she said to Erin and walked toward her. "Will you be his new assistant?"

"Not in the same way," Erin began, mystified by the woman's reaction.

"But in some way," Kimberly said fervently. "You must know that Daniel is a terrific boss. I'm sure he'll be a wonderful king."

The woman's sincere admiration touched a chord inside Erin at the same time as it unsettled her. "Yes, of course, he—"

Kimberly turned to Daniel. "This is amazing. Congratulations. A king. I know a *king*. We are all going to miss you terribly," she said, her voice trembling.

Daniel closed his hands warmly around Kimberly's. "Thank you, but you must keep this confidential," he reminded her.

"I will," she promised solemnly.

"Don't forget to watch out for Justin," Daniel said.

Kimberly paused. "That's going to take some thought," she murmured and turned toward the door. "A king," she whispered. "And Justin…"

Erin watched the astonished woman leave and met Daniel's gaze. She could tell what was coming before he opened his mouth and spoke.

"Say it aloud," he said.

"Must I?"

He nodded.

Erin sighed. "You inspire great loyalty among your employees and family. How do you plan to operate when the political scheme is so different?"

"You mean because I have no one with the same loyalty to me right now in Altaria?"

She slowly nodded.

"Every once in a while you meet a person you know you can trust for life. By the time I get to Altaria, I plan to have at least one person that I can trust," he said and brushed his finger under her chin. "One person who is on my side."

He meant her. Erin's heart contracted. He wanted her trust and loyalty. He had no idea what he was asking.

Six

Erin sat across from Daniel at his favorite noisy downtown diner after a Bulls basketball game. Bloody tired of her conflicting feelings about Daniel, she'd parked her propriety in her hotel room and decided to enjoy the evening and the man. For once, she'd decided to pretend he wasn't the king. She had the uneasy sense that her relationship with him could change more quickly than the Chicago wind whirling outside. A half-consumed American beer sat on the table in front of her, and she was waiting to taste her first Chicago-style hot dog. When in Rome…

"What did you think of the game?" Daniel asked.

"The players were quite tall," she said in an attempt to be complimentary. "And they were very fast with the ball."

"But?" he prompted with his usual intuitiveness. How did he nearly always manage to read her like a book?

"It wasn't very exciting," she confessed. "There were only two fights and those were quickly over."

Daniel stared at her for a long moment, then laughed. "You bloodthirsty woman," he accused.

Erin lifted her chin. "I wouldn't call myself bloodthirsty. I just don't see the entertainment value of watching a bunch of men in baggy shorts running up and down a gym throwing a ball at a basket. There's nothing at stake. In rugby, someone nearly always breaks a bone or gets a tooth knocked out."

He took a long drink of his beer and appeared incredibly amused. "Is there rugby in Altaria?"

Erin winced. "Yes, but I can't say our teams are of a professional caliber." She paused. "In fact, the Brits call us sissies."

Daniel shook his head in disapproval. "That needs to be changed."

The waitress delivered their orders of hot dogs and French fries. "So this is the infamous Chicago hot dog," she said, tilting her head slightly to examine the ingredients. "I'm taking mental notes for the palace chef. It appears to be a beef sausage with mustard, relish, onions, a pickle spear and tomato wedges."

"And celery salt," Daniel added, lifting the hot dog and taking a bite.

"Celery salt," she echoed, watching in dismay as Daniel consumed the messy meal. She looked down at her hot dog and couldn't help wondering how Miss Emily Philpott, her most accomplished head-mistress, would recommend eating such a dish.

"It won't bite you," Daniel told her.

She shot him a dark look. "I know that."

"You don't eat a hot dog with a knife and fork. You're gonna have to get messy," he said. "I dare you."

She caught his green gaze and felt the ridiculous urge to meet his challenge. "Pardon?"

"I dare you to pick up that hot dog with your fingers and take a bite," he said. "A big bite. I bet you can't do it."

She saw through his dare. He was goading her. It would serve him right if she used a knife and fork to spite him. But she wouldn't. Erin deliberately picked up the hot dog and took a large bite. It was incredibly delicious. And incredibly messy. She licked her lips and took another bite, then another.

When she finished, she looked at him and licked her lips again. "I did it," she said, noticing that Daniel was staring at her mouth. She reached for a napkin. "Do I have something on my mouth?"

He shook his head and took a long drink of beer, still seeming fixated on her lips. "Did anyone ever tell you that you have an incredible mouth?"

She automatically licked her lips and heard him groan. "No. I can't say…" The sexual intensity she saw in his eyes snatched the words from her mouth. She felt herself grow warm. His forbidden invitation filled her with anticipation. She felt it in her blood, in her breasts…and lower.

She watched him take another drink of his beer and surreptitiously studied his mouth. She remembered the mind-blowing way he'd kissed her in the closet. Although she'd tried to forget it, the memory never left her alone. She took a careful breath. "That was quite splendid," she managed and took a long drink of beer in hopes of cooling herself off. It didn't work.

"Do you want your fries?" Daniel asked.

Erin shook her head. Her stomach dancing with butterflies, she couldn't imagine eating one more bite.

"Let's go, then," he said and tossed some bills on the table.

Daniel took her arm and led her out of the diner. No sooner had they walked one block toward his parked car than the rain began to pour down. He pulled her into a hotel doorway. "No sense in both of us getting wet. You wait here while I get the car."

Erin immediately shook her head. She didn't want him to think she was a prissy wuss, and besides, for some inexplicable reason, she'd rather get wet by Daniel's side than stay dry without him. "It's not that far. I won't melt," she insisted.

"You sure?" he asked doubtfully.

"Sure," she said and tugged him out into the rain. "Are you too old to run?" she teased.

"Not yet," he returned in a sexy, rough voice and they raced through the rain together. The cold wind whipped through her, and it occurred to Erin that even though she'd endured Switzerland's winters, Chicago's combination of wind and freezing rain chilled her to the bone. By the time Daniel ushered her into his sport utility vehicle, Erin's teeth were chattering.

He dashed inside the car and immediately turned the heat on high. He glanced at her and frowned. "You're shivering. I told you that you should have waited while I got the car."

"It's not that b-bad," she said, her teeth chattering.

"Uh-huh," he said, clearly unconvinced. Daniel quickly drove to his parking deck and hustled her up to his condo. Jordan greeted them with a loud bark at the front door.

Daniel gave the dog a quick pet, then began to peel Erin's jacket from her. "Got to get you warm," he said, rubbing her arms. He ditched his own jacket, led her to the sofa and immediately wrapped an afghan around her shoulders.

His tenderness left her speechless. He lit the gas logs in his fireplace, then sat next to her. "Better?"

She nodded, unable to tear her attention from his eyes. The firelight glowed in them, or perhaps it wasn't the firelight. Perhaps it was his power, more than physical, more than mental. All she knew was that he mesmerized her.

"I like the wet look on you," he said, lifting a damp strand of her hair.

Erin cringed at the thought of her appearance. "I'm sure you do," she said in complete disbelief.

"I'm serious," he said. "I like the way you look right now."

A swarm of emotions whipped through her. She looked anything but perfect, yet he was pleased with her. She glanced at him skeptically. "Why?"

"You look touchable," he said, rubbing her arms with his large hands again.

"I look like a train wreck," she corrected, feeling the same way. She wondered how he did that to her.

"No," he said, meeting her gaze and lifting his thumb to her cheek. "You look like you wouldn't mind being held," he told her. "Or kissed."

Her heart stuttered, and she couldn't look away from his green eyes. He was warm and strong, and he liked her even when she looked like a drowned rat.

She didn't know why or exactly how, but Daniel touched her in a secret place no one else had ever even seen. At that moment, all her defenses evaporated. He slowly leaned forward and closed his arms around her, and Erin had the awesome sense of finding home. The feeling was so strong it brought tears to her eyes. It couldn't be, she tried to tell herself, but as she inhaled his scent and sank into his embrace, heaven help her, but nothing in the world seemed to exist except Daniel.

She felt his heart beating against her and wanted closer. Erin sneaked her arms out from the afghan and slid them around him. They held each other for a long moment, then he nudged her chin upward.

He slowly lowered his mouth to hers. Just a brush of his lips, then he moved back, but Erin could tell he wasn't done.

Her heart hammered in her chest. "Are you sure this is wise?" she asked, clinging to a weak remnant of rational thought.

"Damn right it is," he said, brushing her mouth again, making her pulse skip again. "It's my fault you got cold, so it's my responsibility to get you warm."

She swallowed. "You already have."

"I can make you warmer," he told her and pulled her onto his lap so that she straddled him.

Erin barely had time to react to the impropriety before his mouth took hers and he slid his tongue past her lips. His was a lazy, yet purposeful invasion. He dallied with her sensitive inner lip and toyed with her tongue. She lost herself in the taste and texture of him. Tilting her head to the side to allow him better access, she heard him give a low murmur of approval. The pleasurable sound buzzed through her.

The kiss went on and on as if he couldn't get enough of tasting her. Erin wanted more, but didn't know how.... She felt a rumble of impatience build inside her. Opening her mouth wider, she drew his tongue deeper into her mouth.

Daniel immediately responded, and the tenor of the kiss changed from lazy to serious. She felt his hands slide beneath her sweater to the bare skin of her back.

"Your skin," he muttered. "So soft." His fingers wandered up her ribcage just beneath her bra, and she held her breath. Her breasts strained against the lacy material, but he moved his hands away. She swallowed the frustration nudging at her.

His fingers wandered again to the barrier just beneath her breasts and she held her breath. He slipped one finger beneath the lower band. Back and forth on the lower side of her breast, he moved his finger.

When he removed it, she nearly cried out.

Daniel began to move his tongue in a bold, decadent rhythm that mirrored sex. Erin couldn't withhold a moan.

He moved his hands over her back, and she felt her bra loosen. Then his hands were at last cupping her breasts. Heat pumped through her, making her restless. She shifted on his lap, and he pulled back slightly.

"Do you like this?" he asked, rubbing his fingers ever so lightly on the perimeter of her breasts.

"Yes, but—" She had to fight the urge to arch into his hands.

"Yes, but," he echoed, bringing his fingers closer and closer to her sensitive, erect nipples.

Erin bit her lip and closed her eyes. His thumbs glanced over her stiffened peaks and she moaned again.

He read her response and rubbed her nipples between his thumb and forefinger. A riot of electric sensation coursed through her, and she instinctively took his mouth with hers. She suckled on his bottom lip and dipped her tongue across his.

Daniel took over, French-kissing her until she felt liquid and edgy. Pulling back, he lifted her sweater over her head and pushed away her bra. His gaze greedily drank in the sight of her naked breasts. Tugging his own sweater over his head, he pulled her bare breasts against his bare chest. They both moaned at the sensation.

Firelight danced over the skin of his hard, muscular chest, and the sight of his chest hair arrowing down provocatively into his jeans unwrapped something basic and untapped inside her.

She moved her fingers over his shoulders and chest, luxuriating in the sensation of muscle beneath skin. He cupped her bottom and propped her upward. Dipping his head, he took the tip of her breast in his mouth. The delicious tug of his tongue pulled deep in her nether regions.

Consumed with a want she'd never experienced, Erin glanced down at the sight of his mouth on her breast. The wanton image filled her with shocking pleasure. She had never seen herself as sexy. The notion had been forbidden.

But Daniel's wicked mouth turned all that upside down. She felt him unfasten her belt and unzip her jeans. Her heart beat so hard she couldn't breathe. "What are you doing?"

He dipped his finger beneath her waistband the same way he had touched her breasts just moments ago. "Do you want me to stop?" he asked, his voice easy but his eyes dangerous.

She couldn't honestly say she wanted him to stop.

He dipped his fingers lower then pulled them back. "Do you?"

She would likely burn in hell for everything she was feeling right now, but Erin couldn't bring herself to stop him. She shook her head, and he immediately shifted her so he could push the lower half of her clothes down her legs.

Excitement and nervousness battled inside her. She watched Daniel's eyes devour her body and shivered.

"Cold?" he asked, totally misreading her.

She shook her head as he cupped her bottom and drew her body against his. The denim of his jeans felt rough against her thighs, but his hands were strong and smooth.

"I've wanted to see you this way for a long time," he told her.

"You haven't known me that long," she managed over her hammering heart.

"I've wanted to see you this way since the day I met you. I wanted to do more than look."

At the same time as he took her mouth, he slid his hand down her abdomen between her legs and touched her intimately.

Erin felt a shocking urge and panicked. She pulled her mouth from his and took desperate breaths, praying she wouldn't embarrass herself.

Daniel paused and looked down at her. "Problem?"

She shook her head, but her body gave her away. She hiccuped.

Erin closed her eyes at the nervous habit that had been the bane of her existence. *Why now?* She sucked in another breath and hiccuped again.

"Erin?"

"It's a terrible—" She hiccuped again. "—disability, but I can usually—" She hiccuped. "—make them go away."

"Do you want some water?"

She shook her head. "No. Water doesn't—" She broke off at another spasm. "—work. It must've been my knickers."

He looked at her incredulously. "Knickers?"

Filled with humiliation, she covered her face. "Could you please just give me a moment?"

Daniel did, moving her off his lap and offering her the afghan to cover herself. Erin gratefully covered her body and closed her eyes. It took a few extra seconds, but she conjured the image of a Swiss snowfall. The urge to hiccup subsided.

She reluctantly met Daniel's curious gaze. Her heart rate picked up again. His hair was mussed, his lips swollen from kissing her and his bare chest distracted her. "I can usually keep them under control. Ever since I was a little girl, when I become overexcited, I, uh—" She took a breath and miserably looked away. "I hiccup."

"So you're saying I just got you so overexcited

I made you hiccup?'' Daniel clarified, his voice a combination of astonishment and amusement.

Erin looked at him darkly. ''It's not at all kind to make fun.''

He immediately tugged her onto his lap. ''Who's making fun? You just paid me the ultimate sexual compliment,'' he said. ''But you said something about knickers.''

Still uncertain about his response, Erin felt her cheeks heat. ''Yes, well, I think it happened when you removed my knickers.''

''Knickers,'' he echoed.

''Underdrawers,'' she clarified.

Recognition dawned on his face. ''Ah, well, does this usually happen when your knickers are removed?''

''No,'' she said.

He studied her for a moment. ''Just how often have your knickers been removed?''

''I remove my knickers every day,'' she hedged.

''By a man,'' he added.

She bit her lip and pulled the afghan around her more tightly. ''I'm not sure that's any of your business.''

''Oh, yes, it is,'' he told her. ''Because I want to do a hell of a lot more than take off your knickers.''

Seven

——

Daniel got a sinking feeling as he watched Erin bite her lip for the umpteenth time. "I knew you were inexperienced, but I didn't know you were…" He stopped, his words fading.

"I've been surrounded by women most of my life," she told him. "I've had a few opportunities with men, but—" She broke off and shrugged.

"But what?"

"I never really wanted—" She cleared her throat and her eyes darkened with a hundred feminine secrets he'd like to discover. "There's never really been someone I wanted to get this close to," she said.

Daniel felt his chest and groin tighten. Her revelation made him hard, but her vulnerability touched something deep inside him and made him want to be careful with her. "We haven't made any commitments, Erin," he reminded her as gently as he could.

"Of course not," she said as if the notion appalled her. "That would be foolish with all the changes you're facing."

"Then how do you justify—" He paused. "—letting me in your knickers?"

"I hadn't really tried to examine it too closely," she said. "It's far too complicated, and it's probably wisest not to get close to you, but—"

"But," he prompted.

She met his gaze. "But I want to," she said softly.

His groin and heart tightened further. He hated having to be the rational one when she was giving him an ache that wouldn't quit. He couldn't stop thinking about what she was wearing—or not wearing—underneath his afghan. "I'm much more experienced than you," he said, as much for himself as for her.

"Of course," she said. "I daresay I would have had to start my sexual experimentation at age two in order to match you."

Daniel shot her a dark look for her pointed reference to his age. "Two is an exaggeration," he said dryly.

She arched an eyebrow in disbelief and shifted slightly.

Shifted her naked bottom on his lap. Daniel groaned.

Her gaze holding his, Erin dropped the afghan from her shoulders, baring herself before him.

Daniel drank in the sight of her nakedness, her ivory skin, uptilted breasts, narrow waist and creamy thighs. Oh, how he wanted to slide between her thighs. The temptation was too much to totally resist. He allowed himself to dip his head and taste her. She allowed him access to the inner recesses of her mouth, and Daniel thought about the more intimate access he craved. She would be wet and tight. He shuddered at the thought.

His hands slid over her skin and touched her breasts. Her hardened nipples gratified the hell out of him. Lying back on the couch, he pulled her down with him. He slid his hand down between her legs and found her wet petals with his fingers.

She stiffened.

"I just want to touch you right now," he reassured her. "You feel so good, so wet. Open up for me, baby. Open your mouth," he coaxed her. "Open your legs."

He made love to her mouth while he played with her secrets. He felt her grow swollen, and she began to undulate against him. Her movements were so unconsciously sexy, Daniel began to sweat.

But the little sounds of pleasure she made threatened to make him burst the fly of his jeans. He slid his finger inside her and she nearly cooed. She was close. He could feel it in her small jerky movements. He slid another finger inside her and rubbed her with his thumb.

She gasped into his mouth and stiffened with pleasure. "Oh, Daniel," she said, and the feeling of Erin coming undone sent him to another plane.

Despite the fact that he was so hard he hurt, he held her while she came down. Her breathing settled, and she lifted her eyes to look at him. Her blue eyes heavy with sensual satisfaction, she skimmed her hand down his chest and belly to the belt of his jeans.

Daniel swallowed a growl, and operating against every base instinct he possessed, he covered her hand with his.

"There's more," she said in a sultry voice that slid down his hardness the same way he imagined her mouth would.

"Not tonight," he said, seeing a freezing shower in his future instead of Erin's warm body. "You're not ready," he said, answering her unasked question.

"Pardon me?"

"You're not ready. The rest of tonight would give you hiccups on top of hiccups."

She pulled her hand from his. "I'm not a child."

"I never said you were, but facts are facts. You're small. I'm not. You're gonna feel it the first time."

PLAY THE
Lucky Key Game and get

HOW TO PLAY:

1. With a coin, carefully scratch off gold area at the right. Then check the claim chart to see what we have for you — **2 FREE BOOKS** and a **FREE GIFT** — **ALL YOURS FREE!**

2. Send back the card and you'll receive two brand-new Silhouette Desire® books. These books have a cover price of $3.99 each in the U.S. and $4.50 each in Canada, but they are yours to keep absolutely free.

3. There's no catch. You're under no obligation to buy anything. We charge nothing —ZERO — for your first shipment. And you don't have to make any minimum number of purchases — not even one!

4. The fact is, thousands of readers enjoy receiving books by mail from the Silhouette Reader Service™. They enjoy the convenience of home delivery...they like getting the best new novels at discount prices, BEFORE they're available in stores...and they love their *Heart to Heart* subscriber newsletter featuring author news, horoscopes, recipes, book reviews and much more!

5. We hope that after receiving your free books you'll want to remain a subscriber. But the choice is yours — to continue or cancel, any time at all! So why not take us up on our invitation, with no risk of any kind. You'll be glad you did!

YOURS FREE!
A SURPRISE GIFT

We can't tell you what it is...but we're sure you'll like it! A
FREE GIFT—
just for playing the LUCKY KEY game!

Visit us online at
www.eHarlequin.com

FREE GIFTS!

NO COST! NO OBLIGATION TO BUY!
NO PURCHASE NECESSARY!

PLAY THE
Lucky Key Game

Scratch gold area with a coin.
Then check below to see the books and gift you get!

326 SDL DH25
225 SDL DH2Z

YES! I have scratched off the gold area. Please send me the 2 Free books and gift for which I qualify. I understand I am under no obligation to purchase any books, as explained on the back and on the opposite page.

NAME   (PLEASE PRINT CLEARLY)

ADDRESS

APT.#   CITY

STATE/PROV.   ZIP/POSTAL CODE

| 2 free books plus a gift | | 1 free book |
| 2 free books | | Try Again! |

The Silhouette Reader Service™ — Here's how it works:

Accepting your 2 free books and gift places you under no obligation to buy anything. You may keep the books and gift and return the shipping statement marked "cancel." If you do not cancel, about a month later we'll send you 6 additional books and bill you just $3.34 each in the U.S., or $3.74 each in Canada, plus 25¢ shipping & handling per book and applicable taxes if any.* That's the complete price and — compared to cover prices of $3.99 each in the U.S. and $4.50 each in Canada — it's quite a bargain! You may cancel at any time, but if you choose to continue, every month we'll send you 6 more books, which you may either purchase at the discount price or return to us and cancel your subscription.

*Terms and prices subject to change without notice. Sales tax applicable in N.Y. Canadian residents will be charged applicable provincial taxes and GST.

If offer card is missing write to: Silhouette Reader Service, 3010 Walden Ave., P.O. Box 1867, Buffalo, NY 14240-1867

BUSINESS REPLY MAIL
FIRST-CLASS MAIL   PERMIT NO. 717-003   BUFFALO, NY

POSTAGE WILL BE PAID BY ADDRESSEE

SILHOUETTE READER SERVICE
3010 WALDEN AVE
PO BOX 1867
BUFFALO NY 14240-9952

NO POSTAGE
NECESSARY
IF MAILED
IN THE
UNITED STATES

"Well, I would certainly hope so," she said in a voice bordering on prissy.

Daniel groaned and rose to a sitting position. "Time to get dressed. Time for you to go to your bed and me to go to mine," he said, although he knew he sure as hell wouldn't be sleeping. When she didn't move fast enough for him, he picked up her sweater and pulled it over her head.

She narrowed her eyes at him. "Are you one of those men who tease, then don't deliver?" she challenged.

Her accusation rendered him temporarily speechless. "No, I'm being rational and trying to be a gentleman, but you're making it damn hard. Now get dressed," he said through gritted teeth.

She made a muffled sound of outrage, gathered the rest of her clothes in her arms and flounced toward the bathroom, her delectable rear end taunting him with every step.

Daniel swore under his breath and rubbed a hand over his face. He was doing the right thing. Taking a woman's virginity shouldn't be done lightly. And it wasn't just any woman. It was Erin. Her combination of vulnerability and determination did something to him. He couldn't explain it, but more than anything, he wanted her to trust him and he wanted to be able to trust her.

He pulled his sweater back on and she returned to the room, her hair still a sexy mess, her eyes sparking with a combination of sensuality and anger. "I'll call a cab," she said.

"No," he said, pulling on his jacket and grabbing hers.

"There's no need—"

"There damn well is," he said, holding her jacket out for her.

Wearing a mutinous expression, she jammed her arms into the sleeves and strode with him to the car. During the brief, rainy drive to her hotel, she neither looked at him nor spoke to him.

Daniel suffered in silence until he pulled up to the door. "You were beautiful tonight," he said.

Her eyes looked hopeful, then she glanced away. "Obviously not beautiful enough," she murmured.

"What do you mean by that?"

"I mean, it's a bit humiliating being the only one who got—" She dipped her head. "—who got overexcited."

He stared at her, then glanced heavenward for help. Every swearword he'd ever heard raced through his mind. He counted to ten and turned to her. "Do you really think I wasn't turned on?"

She shrugged. "Not enough to—"

Muttering an oath, he pulled her close to him and kissed her. It was an outrageously carnal, sexual kiss that only revealed the tip of the iceberg of his need. He took her hand and brought it to his still-hard crotch. "Would you say that's excited or not?" he demanded in a low voice.

She met his gaze with surprised eyes.

"I want all the way inside you," he told her. "But I don't want to hurt you."

"How, then?" she whispered.

"We have to take it slow," he said and lifted his hand to stroke her hair. "I'm not walking you up to your room because if I get you anywhere near a bed, you won't walk for twenty-four hours." He pressed his mouth against hers. "Sweet dreams."

Two nights later, Erin folded her hands together to keep from fidgeting, but Daniel must have caught her.

"There's no need to be nervous," he told her, briefly reaching over to cover her hands with one of his as they waited in his SUV at a stoplight. "Most of my family members are friendly."

"I'm sure they are," Erin said. "It's just that I'm eating dinner with the former Princess Emma, and she is so loved by Altaria that she's nearly a legend."

"Why do I suddenly feel like mashed potatoes?" he muttered in a mock-offended tone.

Erin met his gaze and felt the connection between them vibrate from her head down to her toes. The unfinished intimacy they'd shared hovered between them like a steamy summer day. She could no longer deny to herself what an extraordinary man Daniel was, and she was having trouble denying her strong feelings for him in order to keep some sort of perspective.

"You don't need me to tell you that no one could ever think of you as mashed potatoes," she told him.

"No?" He pulled his hand away and turned onto a different road.

"What do you call it? Beef jerky, perhaps?" she suggested, tongue in cheek.

He shot her a dark look edged with amusement. "How far we've come from Your Majesty," he teased.

Chagrined, Erin bit her lip. "You're so right. Forgive me for not showing proper respect."

"Oh no, we're not going to start that again. I was joking with you," he said.

"But you make an important point," she said, and was compelled to add, "sir."

Daniel pulled the car onto the shoulder of the road, put it in park and pulled her against him. He lowered his mouth to hers and took her in a kiss that reminded her of everything they had shared and that intimated everything they hadn't.

He pulled back, and she drew a deep breath in search of her equilibrium.

"I'd say we're past the 'sir' stage, wouldn't you?" he said more than asked.

She nodded slowly. "I suppose, but what about when we go to Altaria? It will be expected—"

"We'll deal with that later," he told her and put the car in gear.

Erin could only nod. She felt a sharp jab of pain in her chest at how everything between them would be forced to change once Daniel made his permanent move to Altaria. She was certain he would take the throne, and he would do so in his own way. Her future wasn't nearly so certain. When her father learned that she hadn't accomplished his plans for Daniel, he would be severely disappointed. If he ever learned that Erin had fallen in— She broke off the terrifying thought. It was enough to bring on a fit of hiccups. Heaven help her, she would deal with all of this when the time came.

Daniel pulled into a long driveway leading to a large, beautiful redbrick Georgian manor home. "Home sweet home," he said.

"It's beautiful, and so large," Erin said.

"Both my parents wanted a big family, so they always knew they would need a large place to house them."

"How many children do they have?" Erin asked, fascinated by the idea of a large family.

"My parents have raised nine in all," he said, and stopped the car in front of the house. "Why?"

"I was just trying to imagine what it must have been like to have all those brothers and sisters. Never lonely," she said.

"Never alone," he corrected dryly. "But I wouldn't trade any of them for all the royal jewels in Europe and neither would my parents, even though each of us pushed them to the edge in one way or another.'' He paused and lifted his hand to touch her hair. ''Kinda like you've pushed me to the edge.''

Erin stared at him in surprise. ''Me? How have I pushed you to the edge? Until you berated me into dropping the appropriate form of address, I've been nothing but proper.''

He grinned and his eyes glinted with wickedness. ''Exactly. Erin, when will you learn I want you in ways that are anything but proper?'' he asked.

Before she had time to respond, he exited the car and rounded the vehicle to open her door. ''Ready?'' he asked, offering his hand.

''Yes,'' she said, although her stomach danced with nerves.

Daniel escorted her to the entrance and rang the bell. A housekeeper answered the door and immediately ushered them inside. The immense entryway featured a spiral staircase that floated up to a second story where a grand chandelier hung from the ceiling. The housekeeper took their coats, and it occurred to Erin that Daniel would likely feel comfortable with the grandeur of the palace.

Emma Rosemere Connelly entered the foyer with innate breeding and grace. She looked at her firstborn with love in her eyes. ''There you are,'' she said, and Daniel immediately embraced her. ''We haven't seen enough of you lately,'' she gently scolded.

"I've been busy preparing for my new job," Daniel told her.

"Of course," she said. "I just know I'm never going to see you once you leave for Altaria."

"Never is an exaggeration. Dad's jet has the capacity to cross the Atlantic," he said and gave Erin an insider wink. "Besides, from what Erin tells me, the people of Altaria would love a visit from the former Princess Emma."

Emma turned her attention to Erin. "Forgive me. I should have greeted you immediately. I can see my son is as incorrigible as ever. He gets that strictly from his father's side. I've been trying to civilize him for years, but there's only so much a mother can do," she said with gentle wit. "I commend you on your fortitude. I was afraid Daniel's stubbornness might send you back to Altaria on the first available plane."

Delightfully surprised by Emma's lack of reserve, Erin couldn't suppress a laugh. "Thank you for your kind greeting. I must confess this assignment has required a great deal of negotiation. Daniel is quite strong-minded."

Emma beamed. "His father often used the term *bullheaded,* but he's certainly one to talk. Strong-minded," his mother mused aloud and threw Daniel an arch glance. "A lovely description. You must have charmed her."

"And the source of all the charm is obviously my mother," Daniel told Erin dryly.

"Obviously," Emma said with a regal smile, then accompanied Erin and Daniel down the hall. "I'm delighted you both could come. I suspect Daniel won't be in Chicago much longer. Erin, I'm sorry you've had to endure one of our toughest months in terms of weather. I remember Altaria's mild climate and often long for those lovely temperatures in winter. Everyone is in the family room," she said as they rounded a corner into a large, comfortably furnished room with wooden paneling and cases of leather-bound books and trophies.

Daniel's father glanced up from his conversation with a young woman and lifted his glass. "Hail to the king," he said with serious eyes and a slight smile.

"Hail to the king," the others chorused, and descended on Daniel.

"When are you leaving?" one young woman asked.

"What are you going to do with Jordan?" a man asked.

Daniel raised his hands and laughed. "Hold on! I'm not sure when I'm leaving, but when I do, Jordan will go with me. In the meantime, I'd like you to meet Erin Lawrence. Erin, you've met Brett."

Erin nodded at Daniel's younger brother.

"That's my brother Drew," Daniel said, pointing to a tall man with Emma's blue eyes. "He's Vice President of Overseas Operations for Connelly and father of a six-year-old computer-whiz daughter."

"Pleased to meet you," Drew said, extending his hand.

"My pleasure," Erin murmured.

"This is my sister Maggie," Daniel continued, hugging a young woman with long brown hair. "She's a graduate student and she's the baby."

"Forever the baby," Maggie said with a moan and eyed Erin curiously. "Forgive my curiosity, but what is your role with his kingliness?"

"She's teaching him royal protocol and etiquette," Brett said, clearly amused.

Maggie winced. "Oh, my. Please accept my condolences."

"Maggie is also a brat," Daniel said.

Perhaps, but a perceptive brat, Erin thought. "I'm delighted to meet you. What are you studying?"

"Business and art," Maggie replied, as if the two fields were obviously related.

"I'm also interested in art," Erin said. "I'd love to hear more about your studies."

Maggie smiled with pleasure. "Maybe I can talk my mother into letting me sit next to you at the dinner table."

"Speaking of which," said a woman with short, chic black hair and sad violet eyes. "I can't stay. Previous dinner date with John Parker."

Daniel raised an eyebrow. "Isn't that one of Dad's business associates?"

"Yes it is," she said and stood on tiptoe to give Daniel a hug. "May you reign in truth, beauty and

safety. Don't work too hard in your new position."
She turned to Erin. "It's so nice to meet you. I'm
Daniel's sister Tara. I'm sorry I can't stay longer."

"I understand," Erin said. "I'm pleased to meet
you, and I hope you have an enjoyable evening."

Tara's eyes flickered with an emotion Erin
couldn't quite name, then Daniel's sister tightened
her mouth. "Thank you. I'll do my best," she said
and turned, waving to Daniel as she headed for the
door. "Take care of yourself, Your Majesty."

He gave her a two-fingered salute and glanced
thoughtfully after his sister. "Will we ever see Tara
the Terror again?" he murmured.

"Pardon?" Erin said.

His mother and father came up behind them.
"Tara lost her husband in a train wreck a couple of
years ago, and she's never quite been the same,"
Emma said, clearly grieved that her daughter hadn't
recovered.

Grant Connelly slid his arm around his wife in
support, but Erin could see a wisp of sadness in his
eyes too. "Someday the fire will return," he said to
Emma.

Erin felt her heart twist with longing at the obvious connection of love and history among the
Connellys. They had no idea how precious that special bond was.

Seeming to pull himself out of his thoughts, Grant
turned to Erin and extended his hand. "We're glad
you could come. Emma would have never forgiven

herself if she hadn't arranged for you to visit. She may have been born a princess, but she's a natural mother, and she couldn't stand the thought of not welcoming you when you're so far from home. She mothers everyone younger than her.''

Emma's cheeks colored. ''Oh, you're exaggerating.''

Grant shook his head. ''Didn't I hear you inviting Marc's daughter to visit?''

''Catherine said she would like to come visit once she gets Marc's affairs in order. Of course I invited her. Catherine is my niece, and I know that losing her father and grandfather has been devastating for her.''

''As your own double loss has been, Mrs. Connelly,'' Erin said quietly.

Emma took her hand. ''What a sensitive young woman. Thank you for your sympathy. Although I'll miss Daniel terribly, I take some solace in the fact that he is carrying on the Rosemere tradition. I'm grateful for any help you may give him in that respect.''

Erin felt a sharp stab of guilt. If Emma only knew that Erin's father wished Daniel wouldn't become king.

''Can I get you something to drink?'' Grant asked, while Erin continued to struggle with myriad feelings.

''You're very kind,'' Erin said, seeing in his father a resemblance of the strength and hospitality

Daniel also showed. "White wine would be lovely, thank you."

A woman appeared in the doorway to announce dinner, and the group filed into a long dining room beautifully decorated with mirrors and paintings.

Maggie sat beside Erin at dinner and they discussed art and Maggie's continuing education. Erin felt an immediate affinity with the youngest Connelly. Throughout the meal, however, she never forgot that Daniel was sitting right next to her. The way he talked and laughed with his family showed his ease with them and himself. Erin was beginning to see that Daniel seemed comfortable in every situation. A man for every man, she thought, watching him for a long moment.

"You're staring," he murmured for her ears only.

Embarrassed, Erin immediately glanced down at the peas on her plate. "I'm sorry," she whispered.

"That's okay. You can tell me what you were thinking after dinner."

She threw him a long-suffering glance.

He grinned. "Maggie might have told you about her art, but has she told you about her penchant for speed?"

Erin glanced at Daniel's sister. "Speed?"

Maggie rolled her eyes. "If I were male, we wouldn't be having this discussion. I drive a Lamborghini. My brothers would rather see me drive something with a little less power."

"It might have something to do with the speeding tickets," Grant interjected.

"I've talked my way out of most of them," she reminded him with a sigh. "I'm really a very safe driver. The car gives a terrific ride if you'd like to go some time," she said to Erin.

Delighted at the prospect, Erin smiled. "I'd love to."

Daniel made a growling sound. "We'll see. Dinner was great as usual. Please excuse Erin and me while I show her around."

The family murmured their temporary farewells and Daniel led her through the hallway and up the spiral staircase. Photos and portraits revealed the family history. Informal royal photos showed the pride of King Thomas and the quiet contentment of Queen Lucinda. Even as a child, Prince Marc's reckless charm glinted in his eyes. Princess Emma's fresh, exquisite beauty almost, but not quite, hid the determination in her gaze. That determination and adventuresome spirit had come in handy when she'd tossed her royal title the same way a bride tosses her bouquet. Erin couldn't help lingering over Grant and Emma's wedding portrait. Daniel told stories about his growing-up years as they walked through the grand house, and Erin could almost feel the love and passion of the Connelly family echoing through the walls. He led her into a small study to a floor-length window and cut the lights.

"Look," he said, pointing outside to a maze of boxwood shrubs lit with thousands of white lights.

To Erin, it looked like a wonderland. "I love it," she said. "How long has it been there? Did you play in it as a child?"

Daniel nodded. "It's been here as long as I have. When we were children, my brothers and sisters and I played hide-and-seek in there all the time. As I grew older, I sometimes went there for the solitude."

Erin felt an overwhelming impulse. "Can we go there right now?"

He looked at her doubtfully. "It's freezing."

"Are you afraid you'll catch a chill?" she goaded innocently.

Daniel's gaze darkened. "Absolutely not. I was thinking of you."

"But you were quite expert at warming me up," she ventured, following another bold impulse.

"Yes, I was," he said, and nudged her toward the door. "Let's get our coats."

Eight

Surrounded by the shrubs, tiny white lights and the cold night air, Erin stood with Daniel in the center of the maze. It was so cold their breaths made puffs of vapor, but the sky was like a black velvet blanket filled with diamonds.

"It's beautiful," Erin said, her voice hushed.

He nodded, putting both his arms around her to keep her warm. "Perfect night for wishing on a star, if you believe in that sort of thing."

Erin looked up at his firm jaw and chiseled features and felt a deep longing to know him. "Do you?"

"Experience has taught me that if you want something to happen, you usually have to make it happen, but I share my father's Irish roots, so I'm not opposed to a little good luck or magic.''

Erin glanced up at the sky and felt a flood of wishes race through her. Secret longings she buried every day. *I wish I'd known my mum longer. I wish my father and I were closer.* Erin's heart twisted. The prospect of her accomplishing what her father had asked grew less likely with each passing day. With Daniel's arms around her, however, she felt safer and less alone than she'd felt in her entire life. She wondered, though, what she could possibly bring to such a strong man. He hardly seemed to need anything, let alone her.

Erin closed her eyes. *I wish I were necessary for him.* She knew it was silly, but she made the secret, futile wish on the brightest star in the sky, thinking that for her entire life she had wanted to be necessary to someone.

''I'm making a wish,'' he told her in a low voice next to her ear.

She opened her eyes, and the glint of passion in his green gaze sizzled through her. ''What is your wish?''

''I want your lips on mine,'' he said.

Standing on tiptoe, Erin pressed her mouth to his and granted his wish, all the while thinking she wanted more with Daniel than this kiss, even if it meant that her father shut her out forever.

The knowledge ripped her reserve to shreds. She slid her hands inside his coat and dipped her tongue inside his mouth. He tightened his embrace around her, and, despite the cold night air, Erin felt warmth suffuse her. She gently sucked his tongue into her mouth and arched her breasts against his chest.

Daniel groaned and pulled his mouth slightly away. Resting his forehead against hers, he took a measured breath. "You're making me wish for a lot more than a kiss."

Erin's heart stuttered. She felt as if she faced a fork in the road, and, once she chose, she would never be able to turn back. She shivered, but the decision echoed inside her like a bass drum. It was so loud she almost wondered if Daniel could hear it. She could no longer deny how strongly she was drawn to him. Even though any woman in her right mind would know she had no future with him, she couldn't not be with him.

Trying to control her pounding heart, she rubbed her open mouth over his in invitation. "You must be wishing on the right star."

The next several moments passed in a blur. Daniel led her back through his family's home to say goodnight, then drove toward his condo. They spoke very little, but his every look was so sexually intense she felt branded. At each traffic light, he reached over and took her mouth in kisses that left her dizzy.

As soon as they entered his condo, he turned to her as if he couldn't bear not to touch her. He shoved her coat off her shoulders and unzipped her dress with mind-robbing speed. Before she could take a breath, he lifted her in his arms and carried her to his bedroom.

Erin felt as if she'd waited her entire life for this moment. He put her down on the bed, grabbed a couple of plastic packets of protection from his bedside-table drawer and shucked his clothes.

She admired his muscular body. When he removed his drawers and she saw the size of his masculinity, a sliver of trepidation scurried through her.

He looked at her through hooded eyes and propped himself on top of her, resting his weight on his elbows. "Are you sure about this?"

Loving the way he surrounded her, she fought a slice of panic. Heaven help her, she didn't want to hiccup. "Yes," she managed over the loud beating of her heart.

"You don't look sure," he said, nuzzling her neck and sending delicious sensations through her nerve endings.

"I'm sure," she insisted breathlessly, arching toward him.

"I wish you weren't wearing a bra," he said, running the tip of his tongue down her throat.

Erin bit her lip and fumbled with the clasp of her bra, freeing her breasts.

His gaze devoured her. "Your breasts drive me crazy," he said. "I can't decide whether to touch them with my hands or take them with my mouth."

Erin felt her nipples turn to stiff buds, and she deliberately shed her timidity. "With your mouth," she suggested, winning a look of aroused surprise from him.

He looked down at her breasts again and lowered his head to lazily lap at one of her nipples. He drew the tight peak into his mouth and she felt a tug all the way down to her blooming femininity.

Shifting restlessly beneath him, she lowered her hands to his head. At the same time he slid his hands down to her bottom, rotating her pelvis against his. The combination of sensations sent a roll of thunder through her.

"I wish I didn't want to go so fast," he muttered, lifting his head.

"I don't want to help you with that wish," she admitted, and he gave a low, sexy laugh that sent a rush of heat through her blood.

"I wish you weren't wearing any stockings," he said.

"Then help me take them off."

His eyes glittering with arousal, he helped her remove them, so that she was completely naked before him. His nostrils flared as he looked at her. He slid his fingers between her legs to where she was wet. "Soft as a rose," he said, toying with her, slipping his finger inside her. "So pretty," he murmured. "Everywhere." He met her eyes. "Touch me."

Her tight chest squeezed the oxygen from her lungs, and Erin lifted her hands to Daniel's chest. She ran her thumbs over his flat nipples, then lower to his belly, then lower still to his thigh.

Daniel watched her through dark, wanting eyes and stayed so very still, as if he were a lion preparing to pounce. She could sense his instinctual need to take her as he slid his finger inside her yet again. Erin felt herself grow swollen with need. With each stroke from his hand, she wanted more and more.

She skimmed her hand up his thigh to his hard masculinity and watched him exhale on a hissing breath. His passion fed hers; he guided her hand around him, gently pumping. A drop of honeyed arousal formed and she rubbed the tip of him with her thumb.

He closed his eyes as if her touch brought him to the point of pleasure/pain. He stilled her hand and shuddered.

He fondled and stroked her femininity until she was breathless, biting her lip to keep from begging him to take her. "I wish," she said, wrapping her fingers around his arms, "you were inside me."

Daniel swore under his breath and quickly put on the protection. Easing her legs apart, he pushed just inside her opening and stopped.

Feeling herself stretch to accommodate him, she wiggled to take in more.

Daniel swore again. "You're not making this easy for me. I want this to be good for you."

Her urgency for him making her restless, she moved again. "You are good for me, but I want—" She broke off when he pushed farther inside her. The stretching sensation intensified.

"Too much?" he asked through gritted teeth as his biceps strained with the force of his restraint.

Erin automatically shook her head. She could never get too much of Daniel.

He thrust past her resistance, taking her breath with his complete invasion. He felt too big, too hard, and it hurt.

For five seconds.

His nostrils flaring, he stared into her eyes. "Tell me when you're okay."

Erin bit her lip and felt her heart twist. "I haven't been okay since I met you," she confessed.

He closed his eyes for a second, then opened them and looked at her with such tenderness she could have wept. "You're such a sweetheart. You make me want to take care of you," he said, then slowly moved. "In every way."

Bending down, he took her mouth the same way he was taking her body. The combination was too erotic, too much for Erin, and a jolt of pleasure sent her over the edge. She felt as if she were free-falling from the sky and just as she started to land, he gave one final thrust and took his own pleasure in her.

Erin had never felt so fulfilled, so complete—almost necessary.

Daniel kept Erin with him the whole night, taking her again in the morning, then pulling her into the shower with him. He would have spent the entire day making love to her again and again, but he didn't want to make her sore. He was acutely sensitive to the fact that she had been a virgin and he was the man who had altered her status forever. He couldn't explain it, but he felt protective of her. She tried to hide her vulnerability, but now more than ever, he knew it was a front. Her trust wrapped around him like silken cord.

Underneath her prissy exterior she was a sensual woman just waiting to come into her own, and heaven help him, he wanted to be around for every discovery she made. Looking down at her naked body, he wanted to take her again. His body grew hard. He felt a possessiveness that surprised the hell out of him.

All along he'd sensed that Erin possessed a loyalty that a man would prize. Daniel wanted the prize, and she had just demonstrated that he had earned a part of it. He craved the rest.

"Why are you staring at me?" she asked.

"I was thinking how beautiful you are," he said, allowing his gaze to roam over her damp hair, lips swollen from his kisses and the rosy tips of her breasts.

"I'm not perfect," she told him.

"I thought we covered the perfection lesson. Even still, I have to disagree," he said, lowering his mouth to one of her nipples. He rolled his tongue over the tip, feeling himself grow hard at the same time she did. "Your nipples fit perfectly in my mouth," he said, and the arousal burned inside him. "Damn, I want you again."

She looked at him from beneath her eyelashes. "Is that so horrid?"

He smiled at her British tone. "No, but it would be horrid if I made you sore."

"Does that mean you can't kiss me?" she asked, wrapping her fingers around his arm and tugging.

Daniel groaned as he lowered his mouth. "No," he muttered as she gave him a French kiss that belied her lack of experience. She slid her hands over his chest and down to his buttocks.

His mind teeming with swearwords, he fought the urge to devour her, to plunge inside her with nothing between them and spill his pleasure inside her. The very thought was so arousing it nearly sent him over the edge.

"How did you become such an incredible lover?" she whispered into his mouth as she lowered her hands to the part of him that ached for her.

"Is it because you've had so much experience?" she asked, and the combination of her words and hands taunted him mercilessly.

"Partly," he managed. "But you motivate me."

"It's not entirely fair that you have all this experience and I have none. I feel the need for more experience," she said, her hands driving him insane.

"You can get experience with me," he told her.

She moved her open mouth down his chest as she continued to caress him. She scorched him when she ran her tongue over one of his nipples, then kissed her way down his belly. Her cheek glanced his hardness, and he bit back a moan.

"Erin, what are you doing?" he asked.

She answered him by touching him intimately with her mouth. He looked down at the sight of her blond hair splayed over his abdomen and her lips on his masculinity.

He didn't know whether to pray or swear, but it didn't much matter. His vocal cords had ceased functioning.

She lifted her smoky gaze to his. "I want to do this right," she said, lowering her head again, "so tell me if I am."

She took him into her oh-so-proper mouth with such enthusiasm and untutored perfection that Daniel had to move her away while he spilled his pleasure. He pulled her head into the crook of his shoulder as he gasped for air.

"You never said if I was doing it right," she ventured.

Daniel could only groan.

Two days later after a call from his brother Brett, Erin watched as Daniel's world began its apple-cart turnover. The media had grown hungry and needed to be fed. It was time for Daniel's first interview as incoming King of Altaria. Her heart burst with pride at his immediate decision to show sensitivity to the citizens of Altaria by conducting an interview to be aired on Altarian television and radio before the American interview. Honoring the line of generational unity to a nation still grieving, his mother appeared with him, but gently demurred for the American interview.

The Altarian reporter was respectful and reserved, the American more hard-hitting, but Daniel appeared confident and in control.

"Why would a successful American businessman choose to accept a primarily superficial role as king of a small, exotic island country?" the American interviewer asked.

"This American chooses to accept the role based on some old-fashioned reasons: family honor and responsibility. I disagree with your view that the role of king is superficial. My understanding is that this job expands and contracts with the individual filling it."

The woman reporter looked surprised. "Is that so? Then do you have any plans for your reign, Your Majesty?" she asked with a great deal of skepticism. Erin felt an overwhelming urge to pinch the woman, but noticed Daniel didn't take the bait.

"It would be wrong for me to enter this role with the notion that I want to change everything. Altaria has succeeded just fine without my ideas for centuries. On the other hand, I would feel irresponsible if I didn't attempt to bring anything new to the table. I'm currently researching the possibility of expanding Altaria's airport. This would improve both tourist and business prospects. I want to explore some possibilities for initiating higher education on the island. I also intend to initiate an audit of all government agencies, including the Rosemere Institute, which my family has funded in the past.''

That reply might give her father indigestion, but Erin found it inspiring.

A Connelly PR person agreed, whispering to her, ''He's excellent. He handles the press as if he were born for the job.''

''He was,'' Erin reminded him, and at the same time, reminded herself that her relationship with Daniel would be changing all too quickly. Her stomach clenched at the thought.

''So you won't be the royal equivalent of an empty suit?'' the woman interviewer said.

Daniel smiled. ''Nothing could be less likely.''

''Tell me about the Rosemere Institute,'' she said.

''The Rosemere Institute was founded by my grandfather, the late King Thomas, to promote technical and medical research. In particular, after my grandmother died of cancer, significant research has been devoted to finding ways to fight cancer.''

Erin watched as Daniel used his everyman charm and intelligence to successfully field the interviewer's questions. His thoughtful sincerity would break down walls. By the end of the session, she had never been more certain that Daniel was the best man to become King of Altaria.

He disconnected his microphone, shook hands

with the interviewer and ran his searching gaze over the studio. "Erin?" he called, making her heart leap.

She waved and he spotted her. Shooting her a private half grin, he quickly joined her. "I'm hungry after that duel with the devil," he murmured for her ears only. "Chicago dogs or pizza?"

"What about security?"

"Tomorrow morning," he said, and she could feel the clock ticking inside her. "We have one more night without an army of Peeping Toms. I'm not wasting it," he promised.

Erin and Daniel filled every minute the rest of the day and into the night. They grabbed a take-out meal of Chicago hot dogs and Daniel fed Erin hers in the most audacious, provocative manner she could have imagined. She paid him back by using her tongue to lick a thin line of mustard all the way up the hot dog. The food was quickly forgotten and they devoured each other.

Rising early, Daniel hustled her in and out of the shower, and they took Jordan for a brisk walk.

"It's a sunny day," he said as he guided her down the sidewalk.

"A freezing sunny day," she said.

"I'll warm you up," he promised with an expression in his eyes that made her stomach dip and sway. He slowed and kissed her.

"You'll be too busy for warming me up," she gently told him. "Many meetings today."

"I'll never be too busy to warm you up, Erin. Don't forget that." He grabbed her hand and began to walk again.

Rounding the corner, Erin heard a loud sound as if a car were backfiring. The sound cracked through the air, and a window just above her shattered. Startled, she looked up.

"Get down!" Daniel cried, shoving her to the ground as another shot rang out. She heard the squeal of tires on the pavement and saw a black car disappear down the street.

Fear raced through her like ice water. She clung to Daniel. "Daniel? Daniel?" When he didn't immediately respond, her heart stopped. She turned his face to hers, and nearly fainted at the sight of his blood-splattered forehead.

Nine

Hours later after the Chicago Police Department had thoroughly questioned Daniel and Erin, and the Connelly men had joined ranks for a private meeting, an official Altarian security guard stood outside Daniel's condo. Erin began to breathe again.

Daniel met her gaze and flipped her hair behind her shoulder. "The bullet barely grazed my forehead."

Erin felt the bile rise in the back of her throat. "You were bleeding. You were hurt."

He pulled her into his arms. "You could have been too."

"You saved my life," she told him, tears welling up in her eyes. "I've never been so frightened in my life.'' What if he'd been hit? What if she'd truly lost him? Even though she knew he would never belong to her, Erin couldn't bear the thought of his death. She began to tremble.

Daniel pulled slightly away and frowned. ''You're shaking,'' he said. ''You must stop. You're okay and so am I.'' His expression shifted. ''And it's been decided that you and I will return to Altaria tomorrow.''

Erin searched his gaze. ''Who made the decision? Security?''

''Security, the Connelly men and me. It's time for me to take the next step in the transition. I might like to pretend that this was a random drive-by shooting, but...'' He drifted off, shaking his head.

''But it's entirely too coincidental that your interview was aired internationally last night and you were shot at in broad daylight this morning.''

He nodded slowly. ''For some reason, someone doesn't want me to be king.''

Her heart twisted. She thought of her father, but knew he wouldn't go to such lengths. ''Why?'' she wondered aloud.

''I don't know. I can't spend time thinking about detractors. There's too much else I need to be doing. Security will do their job,'' he said.

Erin shook her head. ''You could have lost your life. How can you shake this off so easily? Doesn't this give you second thoughts about becoming king?''

"No," he said with a determination in his eyes that could bend steel. "In fact, it makes me more certain than ever. Several people have been telling me this is a cream-puff job with the emphasis in my role on decorum. No real power to the position. No opportunity to make a difference. If there's no real power, then why does somebody want to kill me?"

Erin joined Daniel and several official security guards on a chartered jet bound for Altaria the following day. She had no idea what would happen once they arrived at the island. She only knew that things between her and Daniel were about to change in a drastic way.

They arrived late at night, as planned, with the goal of a low-key entrance. Word, however, must have gotten out, for a huge crowd of people and several official vehicles stood outside the airport waiting. The people waved welcome signs and cheered.

"You'll walk with me," Daniel said to Erin.

"Absolutely not," she said.

He blinked at her immediate disagreement. "Why not? Other than, 'It wouldn't be proper.'"

"That should be enough," she told him, her heart twisting in strange ways. "I don't want you facing any questions from the press regarding me."

"After that barracuda in Chicago, I can handle nosey questions from anyone."

"I insist," she said quietly.

He jammed his hand into his pocket impatiently. "You're going to be prissy about this, aren't you?"

"I prefer the word *firm*," she said and gently smiled. "You must meet your subjects. You represent their tie to the past and their hope in the future. Your very presence will be a tremendous source of comfort."

"Okay. But you have to come to the palace."

She shook her head.

"I'm not budging on this. If you need a job description, you are palace liaison, and your first duty is to escort Jordan to the palace and get him settled. I'm told he won't need to be quarantined."

Erin gaped at Daniel. "Jordan?"

Daniel nodded, pulling on a suit jacket. "That's appropriate. I want at least two on my side at the palace round the clock. That would be Jordan and you." He leaned toward her and kissed her. "Any last-minute protocol instructions? Is my tie straight?"

With numb fingers, Erin adjusted his tie. Daniel might fight it, but this was the beginning of the end for them. "Give them a chance to bow or curtsey. They want to show respect." A myriad of feelings tugged at her. "You are going to be a wonderful king," she told him.

His gaze grew serious. "I'll see you later at the palace."

Jordan wasn't particularly cooperative. Erin was forced to send a guard to secure a steak to bribe the

beast to go along with her. She gave up trying to
return him to the crate in which he'd made the trans-
atlantic journey. Growling at every new human who
crossed his path, Jordan finally settled down and
stayed close to Erin as the limo left the airport and
traveled toward the palace.

When he pawed at the window, she lowered it
slightly.

The security guard frowned in disapproval.

"He's upset," she said. "He's had a rough couple
of days."

Jordan spent the remainder of the ride panting and
intermittently whining. He clearly wanted Daniel.
Erin couldn't blame him. After they arrived at the
palace, she took him for a short walk so he could
take care of his business. By the time she was ready
to take him inside, Daniel's motorcade had pulled
into the private compound.

Jordan perked up his ears as the vehicles ap-
proached. When Daniel stepped from his vehicle,
Erin nearly got whiplash holding Jordan in place.
The animal began to whine and bark.

Daniel glanced up and spotted them. "Bring him
over," he called.

Jordan dragged her along until they reached his
master, when he began to whine and jump for joy.
Daniel petted him and murmured words of reassurance. He nodded up at the medieval stone palace,
then glanced at her. "Looks like we should be able

to squeeze in a royal protocol expert and palace liaison.''

"Sir," she said, all too aware of the watching eyes all around them.

"Don't start with that," Daniel said.

"I must," she whispered. "At least when others are around. It's expected."

He frowned, clearly not pleased. "I don't like it," he said.

"If you'll pardon me for saying so, sir, you don't have to like it."

"I'm not in the mood to pardon much of anything, so let's go ahead and get past the goons," he muttered, waiting for her to join him.

"You must precede, sir," she reminded him.

Daniel swallowed a half dozen swearwords. He would adjust to the changes. He'd long ago learned the power of the ability to adapt. After the events of the last few days, Erin had to play royal subject for the sake of prying eyes. It bothered the hell out of him that they had to hide their true relationship, even though he understood the wisdom behind it.

A doorman greeted him with a polite bow, and Daniel shook his hand, almost surprising the starch out of the man. A palace guide led him through the castle. Although he was weary, he took in the sight of the lavish decorations and medieval unicorn tapestries, the red-tiled floors carpeted with Oriental rugs.

Daniel waited for a bow or curtsey, then shook hands with the next fifteen palace personnel. When he was introduced to the senior housekeeper, he requested a room for Erin.

Reaching his private quarters, he sent the guards and palace personnel away, and insisted Erin bring Jordan with her into his private domain. Ditching his jacket and tie, he prowled his surroundings. The formal sitting room was decorated with fine period furniture. It needed light, he thought, then wandered into a study with shelves of leather-bound volumes and a beautiful large desk his grandfather must have used.

Daniel's gut twisted at the image of his grandfather and all the Rosemeres before him sitting at that desk. He felt the weight of his title settle on his shoulders. His grandfather descended from a long line of Rosemeres who had ruled with compassion. Daniel was determined to continue the tradition, to continue the honor.

Out of the corner of his eye, he noticed Jordan exploring his new surroundings, sniffing every inch of the place. He glanced up and saw Erin foraging in a small refrigerator. The sight of her eased the upheaval inside him.

"Would you like a sandwich?" she asked. "It appears someone stocked the refrigerator in anticipation of your arrival. Looks like ham, turkey, roast beef and cheese."

Thank God she'd ditched the sir. "I wish for a kiss," he said, and she turned to meet his gaze.

She looked soft and beautiful and like everything he'd never known he wanted but had needed.

She smiled and walked toward him, and Daniel felt the weight of the day grow lighter.

"A kiss. I can do that," she said, stretching on tiptoe to press her soft mouth to his.

Daniel closed his arms around her and savored the sensation of her body against his.

A knock sounded at the door, and he groaned. "I told them to go away."

Jordan barked at the door. "You should answer," she told him, nuzzling Daniel's cheek, then backing away. "I'll hold on to Jordan."

Daniel opened the door to a tall, reed-thin man with a receding hairline. "Your Majesty," he said. "My name is Gregor Paulus, Prince Marc's former assistant. I beg you to forgive the intrusion. I was unable to meet you earlier because I was ordering a tray for your arrival. May I come in, sir?"

Although the man was politeness personified, something about him seemed pushy. Daniel put the first impression down to weariness and set it aside. "Thank you very much, Gregor."

Gregor stepped inside the door. When Jordan barked at him, the man nearly dropped his tray. Daniel rescued it in time.

"Gregor Paulus, this is Erin Lawrence, my protocol expert and palace liaison, and my dog, Jordan.''

Gregor nodded at Erin and murmured a polite greeting. He glanced at Jordan and gingerly extended his hand to the dog's head. Daniel immediately concluded that Gregor was not a dog person.

Keeping one eye on Jordan, Gregor moved to the other side of the room. "I wanted to greet you personally, Your Majesty,'' he said. "I know you will be making many adjustments and I want you to know that I am at your service to help you in any way, day or night.''

Daniel considered asking the proper man to walk his dog, but he didn't want to put Jordan in misery. "I appreciate your kind offer,'' Daniel said instead. "If I should need you, I will call. It was very kind of you to prepare the food. Tonight I plan to retire as soon as possible.''

Gregor nodded, still glancing at Jordan. "Very good, sir. You are most welcome. Again, if you should need anything, anything at all, please do not hesitate to call me,'' he said and backed out of the door.

As soon as the man left, Daniel turned to Erin. "Is it just me or was that guy a little overboard?''

"He was extremely proper and respectful,'' she said and paused. "Oh, all right. Something about him gave me the willies.''

"And he didn't like Jordan,'' Daniel added.

"You can tell a lot about a person by whether they like dogs."

"I technically don't own a dog," Erin pointed out.

"Yes, but you want one," Daniel said and grinned. "Poodles are prissy, but they're still dogs. And Jordan likes you."

"He likes me when I have food," she corrected.

"I want you to stay in my room tonight," Daniel said, expecting a disagreement as he moved toward her.

Erin shook her head. "It's not proper. It wouldn't be right. Heaven forbid the palace aides start talking right away," she said. "I cannot allow you to—"

Daniel pressed his mouth over hers, swallowing the rest of her protests. He kissed her with the passion and frustration from his day. He claimed her mouth in blatant possessiveness, and her objections finally died.

The phone rang the following morning just as Erin and Daniel finished eating breakfast in his private quarters.

Daniel frowned. "Damn, this better not be happening all the time, or I'm gonna have to make this number unlisted to everyone." He picked up the phone. "Hello."

"Daniel," It was his brother Brett.

"Right here," Daniel said, hearing a mixture of impatience and tension in his brother's tone.

"It's about time. This is my third try, but they wouldn't let me through because His Majesty was sleeping."

Daniel winced. "I'll have to tell them to allow calls from my family members," he said and mouthed Brett's name in response to Erin's look of inquiry. "What's up?"

"Nothing good, but we're working on it. We're beginning to think that King Thomas and Prince Marc may have been murdered."

Daniel's blood turned to ice. "What?"

"Yeah, we don't think the boating accident *was* an accident, so we're hiring an investigator. His name is Albert Dessage. He's based in France and he'll be coming to Altaria. We've also got a detective, Elena Delgado, in the Special Investigative Unit of the Chicago Police Department to look into that little drive-by that happened to you."

Daniel took a moment to allow his brother's announcement to sink in. He wondered why. Why would someone have wanted to kill King Thomas? Daniel had never been close to his maternal grandfather, but he'd always gotten the impression King Thomas had been a proper king with integrity to spare.

"You still there?"

Daniel rubbed a hand over his face. "Yeah, I'm just trying to figure out whom I can trust here."

"Watch your back," Brett said.

"I will," Daniel said. He might not have chosen

this situation, but he was determined to deal with it effectively. He suspected it wasn't the first trying situation he would face as monarch.

"And take pity on me," Brett added in a lighter tone. "I've been appointed to deal with the female detective."

Daniel grinned. "Why should I feel sorry for you, you dog? Something tells me you'll use that situation to your advantage."

"Ms. Delgado's probably a battle-ax. Besides, it's easy for you to say. You've got the pretty blonde with the sexy accent."

Daniel smiled at Erin. "I need some consolation."

"Yeah, right," Brett said in disbelief. "How's the palace?"

"Old, dark and the pipes rattle in the shower," he said. "But the temperature is seventy-three degrees and the view of the beach is great."

"It's fourteen degrees and snowing here."

Daniel laughed. "Come and visit."

"I can't. I've got to deal with the battle-ax. I better run. I meant what I said about you watching your back."

Daniel heard the heartfelt sincerity in his brother's voice and it warmed him. "I will. Thanks. Keep me posted."

Daniel hung up and met Erin's curious gaze. He crossed the room to her and took her in his arms. "I'm glad you're here with me," he said.

Her eyes widened. "Why?"

"Because the more I learn about things in Altaria, the less I think I can trust people. I know I can trust you."

Erin took a quick breath and looked downward. "Surely it can't be that bad. There must be others you can trust."

Daniel gave a laugh edged with gallows humor. "I'll be okay, but it's tricky right now. There's a strong possibility that King Thomas and Prince Marc were murdered. Add in the attempt on my life and it's not pretty."

She met his eyes again in disbelief. "King Thomas murdered?" She shook her head. "That's horrible. If it's true, then the same people might want you dead." The color drained from her cheeks and her eyes filled with fear. "Daniel, you must be very careful."

"I will be," he assured her, touched by the strength of her concern. When he had first met Erin, he never would have predicted that the prickly, proper woman could have such an impact on him. She was too young, too inexperienced. Now being with her felt nothing but right. He looked into her blue eyes and wondered if she knew she was becoming more and more important to him every day.

"King Thomas didn't get out among the people of Altaria frequently. He demonstrated the dignity and tradition of the throne in formal state appearances,'' the prime minister told Daniel during their first meeting in the palace's cabinet room. Daniel found himself surrounded by a dozen aides associated with either the PM or the palace.

''I agree that the state appearances are important for the people,'' Daniel said, thinking that if he heard the prime minister say ''King Thomas did it this way'' one more time, he was going to break a piece of the antique furniture. ''Because the citizens of Altaria are less familiar with me, I believe it would be wise to provide a greater degree of accessibility. They need to get to know me and I need to get to know them.''

Louis Gettel, the reserved, intelligent middle-aged prime minister, cleared his throat and adjusted his tie. ''May I inquire how you intend to get to know the citizens of Altaria, sir?''

''I'd like to visit some schools and farms. I'd like to invite some business owners to the palace to talk about their concerns,'' he said, and watched Louis's left eye twitch. Daniel considered joking about the fictional palace orgies he had planned to celebrate spring, but he bit back the audacious urge. ''In the meantime, I've asked a friend to study the possibility of expanding the landing strip at the airport, and I am requesting a full financial and security audit of all government agencies, including the Rosemere Institute.''

Louis nodded. ''Your request will be honored, sir. Your assigned aides will—''

"I'll be interviewing for my own aides," Daniel said.

Louis lifted his eyebrows. "As you wish, sir."

"Mr. Gettel, may I speak frankly?" Daniel asked.

Surprise crossed the man's face. "Of course, sir."

"By all accounts, you are a superb prime minister. Altaria is fortunate to have you in its service," Daniel said.

"Why, thank you, sir," he said, clearly pleased and relieved at Daniel's observation.

"I have no interest in being prime minister of Altaria, and I am not King Thomas, but I do want to be the best damn king I can be."

Gettel blinked, as if Daniel presented one surprise after another. Daniel saw a sliver of wariness leave the man's eyes. His mouth eased into the slightest smile. "We can ask for no more, sir."

Daniel extended his hand and Gettel's shake was strong and sincere. Daniel felt a flicker of hope that his transition wouldn't be a complete walk through hell after all.

After the meeting, Daniel wandered through the palace in search of Erin. He wanted to tell her about his first meeting with the prime minister. Rounding a corner, he thought he heard her talking to someone in a parlor near the entrance of the palace. As he drew closer, the voices became clearer.

"I'm glad you're back in Altaria, safe and sound," a man said. "It appears that you have been successful with your assignment."

Erin's father. Daniel's curiosity was piqued. He walked toward the parlor to meet the foreign minister.

"Father, I don't think—" Erin began.

"You needn't be modest, darling. It's clear you've made yourself indispensable. I'm sure you've rid his mind of any substantial changes he may have wanted to make."

Daniel slowed his steps, frowning.

"Father, I truly don't believe—"

"If you couldn't find a way for the American to refuse the throne, you've obviously done a smashing job of bringing him to heel," her father said. "Just as I instructed you."

Daniel absorbed the man's words. Had there been some kind of plan? Had Erin been scheming against him? The prospect of her betrayal burned like battery acid.

"Father, Daniel Connelly is—"

"I'm so proud of you," Erin's father said.

Daniel's stomach turned. Anger roaring inside him, he strode into the parlor and immediately locked his gaze with Erin's.

She gave a start and paled, her eyes shimmering with guilt.

Daniel's heart twisted to shreds. He glanced at her father, and bitterness backed up in his throat. "Foreign Minister Lawrence, we haven't met. My name is Daniel Connelly."

Erin's father, a thin, short, slightly balding man,

tried unsuccessfully to conceal his horror. He gave a deep bow. "Your Majesty."

"Damn right," Daniel said. "Just for the record, your daughter may have succeeded in making herself indispensable, but no one except my father has ever brought me to heel, and he would tell you he had a hell of a time doing it."

He flicked an icy gaze over Erin. "It appears I misplaced my trust," he said, then left the room.

Ten

Her heart crowding her throat, Erin raced after Daniel. She heard her father calling her as she left.

"Erin!" he said. "Come back here immediately."

She barely spared him a thought. She couldn't pretend to agree with her father one more second, even if it cost her the relationship with him she'd craved. Her heart and mind were with Daniel. The deep betrayal on his face had scored her soul. He had been bitterly disappointed, and she was responsible.

"Daniel," she called as she ran to catch up with him. He didn't pause as he neared his private quarters. "Daniel, *please*—let me explain."

He slowly turned and looked at her with such contempt it took her breath. The only sound between them was her harsh breathing from running.

"Two minutes. I have another appointment," he said and opened the door to his quarters.

Two minutes! Following him into his quarters, Erin panicked and felt the threat of hiccups. Not now, she told herself. Not now when she needed to explain everything to Daniel.

He turned to face her with a stony expression.

She took a deep breath. "I know the conversation with my father must've sounded quite damning, but you didn't hear everything."

"I'm not sure I want to," Daniel said, crossing his arms over his chest.

Erin bit her lip. "Well, you must. It's true that my father asked me to talk you out of taking the throne. He is afraid of change, and since you're American, he feared you wouldn't be at all suitable to be Altaria's king. It's also true that I very much wanted to please my father because we've never been as close as I'd like, so I intended to discourage you from the throne. Once I grew to know you, though, I disagreed with my father." Erin wrung her hands. "It was very distressing to me. I felt disloyal to him. Then I felt disloyal to you."

"You don't need to feel distressed anymore, Erin," he said in a voice so cold it reminded her of the winter weather in Chicago. "Your game is out in the open now. You're just like everyone else. I know I can't depend on you.''

Erin's heart cracked. She closed her eyes. He was so very wrong, but how in the world could she convince him? ''Do you wish me to leave the palace?'' she asked, fighting tears.

''That's up to you,'' he said as if he couldn't care less.

His attitude felt like a knife plunging into her. ''Since I'm more familiar with some of your tastes than most, I believe I should try to ease your transition as much as possible.''

''Your choice,'' he said, glancing at his watch. ''If you'll excuse me, I have an appointment.''

Erin felt her heart sink to her feet. Her two minutes were over, and so was her golden time with Daniel. Feeling lost, she left his quarters, returned to her room and sat down on the bed. She ran her fingers over the beautiful coverlet and felt her eyes well with tears.

How had everything gone so wrong? She had known all along that it wouldn't end well, she reminded herself. Even if Daniel hadn't overheard that terrible one-sided conversation with her father, he was king and he would be obligated to choose a different kind of woman for his bride.

But she had never felt so safe, so wanted, as she had with him. An image of his angry face flashed though her mind and she flinched. She wrapped her

arms around herself for comfort, but the terrible
emptiness inside her only grew wider and deeper.

Erin felt tears burn down her cheeks, and she
couldn't stop a hiccup, then another. Sobbing, she
gave in to the spasms until she was exhausted.

He would never hold her again. He would never
look at her with light in his eyes again.

The reality brought fresh pain and tears. She
rubbed her wet cheeks with the backs of her hands.
The phone on her bedside table startled her with its
ring. She hiccuped, wondering who it might be.
Daniel? Wishful thinking. Her father? She hiccuped
again and decided not to answer. Erin couldn't talk
to her father. She was ashamed she had ever agreed
to try to dissuade Daniel from the throne, and she
couldn't pretend otherwise. Her father would be fu-
rious with her disloyalty.

Her throat tightened. She had lost both Daniel and
her father. Strangely enough, the loss of her father
bothered her far less than the fact that she had
brought Daniel such pain.

Daniel was incredibly strong, but he was making
a difficult transition in Altaria, and she had made it
harder. He had been so angry, so cold. She could
only imagine how betrayed he must feel.

Erin sighed, hiccuping again. The spasms irritated
her, so she turned her attention to getting rid of
them. She pictured a peaceful Swiss snowfall. She
continued to hiccup and frowned.

Closing her eyes again, she allowed her mind to

drift to a different image. A cold, starlit night where she stood with Daniel in the middle of boxwoods lit with tiny white lights. Her heart hurt at the image, but she would never forget the magic they'd shared there that night.

Her hiccups faded and she opened her eyes.

Daniel would never love her. That would be a pain she would endure until she died. But she had the power to make life a little easier for him at this moment. She knew him as no one else in Altaria did. A seed of determination grew inside her.

After a long afternoon spent in meetings with a host of government officials, Daniel sought the solace of his private quarters. Loosening his tie, he entered and found Erin at his desk.

Suspicion immediately burned through him. "What are you doing?" he asked quietly.

Erin looked at him uncertainly. "Moving you in, Your Majesty," she said, lifting her hand to books she'd placed on a shelf.

Daniel gave the books a second look. They were the ones he'd brought with him from Chicago. He relaxed a millimeter.

"I knew you would immediately be plunged into meetings and royal duties, so I thought it best that I go ahead and unpack some of your things. You might not feel quite so out of place that way, sir," she said, arranging one of several photographs of his family. "Does this suit you, sir?"

Even now, when he was still bitter over her betrayal, her formal address grated on him. He glanced over the curves of her body and remembered how she had felt in his arms. Despite his anger, a forbidden flame of arousal flared through him. Disgusted with himself, Daniel looked away.

"It's fine," he said. "Thank you."

He heard her sigh and met her gaze. In her eyes, an expression of hurt and loss came and quickly went. Her hands fluttered nervously before she clasped them together. "I took the liberty of ordering a meal for you, sir," she said. "One of the aides projected the ending time for your meetings and I thought you might be hungry."

"Correct again," he murmured, spotting the covered silver tray behind her.

"Very good, sir," she said briskly. "I've left you Altaria's newspaper, *The Altarian Chronicle,* along with the *Wall Street Journal.* I've arranged for delivery of the Chicago newspaper, but you won't begin receiving that until next week. In the meantime, the palace is equipped with a television satellite with over two hundred channels and you'll be pleased to know one of them is a Chicago station. I've also arranged for some of the palace groundskeepers to build an outdoor run for Jordan. Now, if I may excuse myself, I'll leave you to enjoy your dinner while it's warm."

Daniel blinked at the list of all Erin had accomplished. Curiosity burned alongside his sense of betrayal. "Why?" he asked.

She met his gaze. "Why what, sir?"

"Why did you do all this?"

She shrugged. "As palace liaison, it's my job to make sure you are as comfortable as possible."

"It was also your job to persuade me not to take the throne, or at the least to have me accept that my position was one of decorum only," he said, to keep the edge from his voice.

She paled and took a careful breath as if she'd just been struck. "I obviously was not well-suited for that assignment, sir," she said. "Perhaps I was ineffective because I didn't remain in agreement with it. I hope I will be much more successful with my current assignment." She gave a small, perfect curtsey. "Enjoy your dinner, sir," she said and left.

His heart pounding with a terrible mix of emotions, Daniel closed his eyes. Her light flowery scent lingered in the air. He inhaled deeply and the image of her sweet and naked in his arms invaded his mind. He swore under his breath and opened his eyes.

Her touch lingered just like her scent. His family's photographs had never felt more valuable to him. Seeing his books on the shelf alongside his grandfather's made him feel less like an outsider. It was as if Erin had known exactly what would ease him. He wondered if she was trying to win back his trust.

Daniel immediately rejected the possibility and contemplated whether he should dismiss her. After all, he knew he would never trust her. He was appalled with himself that he'd allowed her to become so important to him.

His stomach churned with a combination of hunger and dissatisfaction. Determined to set thoughts of Erin Lawrence aside, he walked toward his dinner tray and lifted the heavy sterling top. A man's dream meal. Rare steak, new potatoes and green beans. He took a long drink from the cold bottle of beer on the tray and brought his plate with him to the sofa. He reached for the remote and noticed that the first channel on the television was a Chicago station. It was as if she'd been determined to provide him reassurance and comfort in every way.

His heart tightened at the thought, but Daniel would never forget her father's damning words. Never in a million years.

Daniel was in constant motion from the time he rose until late in the evening for the next two days. Each night he found a cold beer waiting for him along with an addition to his private quarters. The latest was a basketball hoop hooked over the wastebasket beside his desk.

Tonight he'd attended a private dinner party at the prime minister's home. Exhausted, all Daniel wanted was to sink into the comfort and privacy of his quarters. But as he entered his suite, he noticed

Jordan was missing. Frowning, he glanced out into the hallway.

Gregor Paulus approached him and bowed. Damn, if the man didn't always seem to be hovering nearby. "Good evening, Your Majesty. May I help you?"

"I'm looking for my dog."

Gregor twitched slightly. "I believe Miss Lawrence took him for a walk. She said he was barking and seemed lonely. Shall I collect them?" he asked, but didn't appear to relish the prospect.

"No, that's okay. I could use a walk myself," Daniel said and strode down the hall. He didn't want to see Erin, he told himself as he exited the palace through a side door. Even though he hadn't seen Erin during the last two days, he didn't miss her at all. He just wanted to see Jordan. He couldn't care less about seeing a certain shapely blonde with transparent blue eyes and warmth to spare beneath her cool English accent.

Daniel heard her before he saw her.

"You're going to be just fine," she said in a low, comforting voice. "You'll see. Your run will be ready in another day and you can play outside and dig holes and drive the palace groundskeepers crazy."

He couldn't stop a flicker of amusement at the sight of Erin sitting on the grass beside Jordan, petting him as she talked to him.

"The only thing is that you may need to mind

your manners a bit when His Majesty entertains special guests." She sniffed. "And I do believe you could use a bath and some mint-scented doggy treats."

"Royal dog walker too?" Daniel asked, and watched both Erin and Jordan whip around to see him. Jordan barked and jumped to his feet, wagging his tail. He jolted forward, jerking Erin along with him.

Daniel bent down to rub his faithful pet. "Rough day, big guy? Mine was jam-packed," he said, then found he was unable to delay looking at Erin one second longer. The incongruous sight of her dressed in a pink ultra-feminine dress with her hands wrapped around Jordan's leather leash in a death grip did something to his gut. Indigestion, he told himself. "You can let him loose from his leash."

Her blue gaze was full of doubt. "Are you sure, sir? I've had difficulty retrieving him a few times."

This was news to him. "How many times have you taken him out?"

"Several, sir. He whines and barks when you're gone."

He nodded slowly, not wanting to be moved by her attentiveness to his dog, of all things. "You can let him go. He'll come when I whistle."

"I should learn how to whistle," she murmured to herself and let Jordan free. The dog immediately raced across the lawn.

Watching Jordan gallop over the grass, Daniel

stood beside Erin. He was acutely aware of her presence and it irritated him. "Just out of curiosity, how have you been collaring him?"

"I've seduced him with steak, sir," she admitted.

The word *seduced* immediately conjured a slew of passionate images in his mind.

"It didn't take much," she continued. "Just a bite or two. The chef has been amenable so far, but I'd better not push it. If I didn't know better, I'd say Jordan laughs at me when I order him to return."

Daniel felt another sliver of amusement at the mental picture. He lifted his fingers to his lips and whistled sharply. Jordan immediately loped toward him and sat in front of him with his tongue hanging out, panting.

Erin stared at Daniel. "That's quite amazing, Dan—" Erin bit her lip at the slip. "Sir," she quickly corrected. "Would you mind showing me how you do that?"

Daniel repeated the whistle at a lower volume.

Jordan cocked his head.

Erin moved closer to study Daniel's mouth. "So you put your index fingers at each corner of your mouth." She lifted her fingers to her lips. "What do I do with my tongue?"

A blazing hot memory roared through Daniel and he bit back a groan. He could tell her several things she could do with her tongue. Tamping down his rampant arousal, he tried to focus on whistling.

"You make a V with your tongue and press it against your bottom lip, then blow."

Erin blew, but didn't produce a whistle. She frowned in consternation and tried again.

Daniel studied her pink mouth and lifted his hand to her jaw. "Try again," he coached. "And press your tongue against your bottom teeth."

Erin tried again and sighed in self-disgust. "I think I may need to practice."

"You didn't learn how to whistle in finishing school," Daniel said, unable to keep a chuckle from his voice.

"There were a lot of things I didn't learn in finishing school," she murmured, her gaze tangling with his.

Daniel's stomach twisted at the sensual awareness on her face. He had put that there, he realized. He had been the man to teach her what a woman couldn't learn in an all-girls finishing school. A primitive possessiveness snaked through his blood, taking him off guard. Lord help him, even though she'd betrayed him, he still wanted her.

The following day, Erin received a request to appear in one of the royal meeting rooms. She wondered if Daniel had instructed his chief of staff to fire her. The prospect filled her with a mixture of dread and relief. Although she hated the idea of losing her accessibility to him, she welcomed the possibility that she would no longer have to endure his anger or disdain.

Entering the room, she saw several palace aides, royal security, and Daniel's chief of staff already waiting. Erin approved Daniel's choice for his chief of staff, Anthony Muller. She'd thought Daniel might choose Gregor Paulus simply because the man was so ingratiating, but she should have known better. Daniel was his own man. He would choose the man he believed best for such a crucial position. Anthony Muller was slightly older than Daniel and had acquired his college education in the United States. To put it in crude terms, Anthony was no suck-up. When asked for the truth, he spoke it.

Anthony nodded toward her in greeting, then turned his attention to the crowd. "Okay, everyone. You'll be honored to know that you have been selected to join His Majesty on his first official outing this afternoon."

Low murmurs of excitement traveled through the room. Erin felt a ripple of surprise and wondered why she had been chosen. Perhaps Daniel planned to bring Jordan along and he wanted a companion for his dog, she thought wryly.

"Some of you have heard about the fires that recently destroyed several farms. His Majesty plans to visit the farmers in a show of moral support. We will depart promptly at thirteen hundred hours," Anthony said. "Meet here fifteen minutes prior to that for further instruction." As he dismissed the group, he gestured toward Erin, who met him in the door-way.

"His Majesty requires your services as protocol consultant on this visit," Anthony said.

Erin nodded, still surprised Daniel would want anything from her.

A couple of hours later she joined Daniel in his private quarters. He was stewing over his wardrobe. "It's ridiculous to wear a suit to a farm when the temperature is above eighty degrees."

"I agree, sir," Erin said. "Ridiculous, but nec-essary. After all, this is your first planned public appearance in Altaria, and it's best to project a royal image."

He frowned at her. "Don't tell me I'm supposed to wear a crown for this," he said.

"Of course not, sir. You won't receive your crown until the coronation. The press will be out in full force today."

"I plan to shake hands with everyone I meet," he warned her.

"That's fine. Just give them an opportunity to show their respect first," she said, then impulsively added, "I think you've made a splendid choice for your first outing, sir. The citizens you greet today will be quite honored by your presence."

"A new barn might be more welcome," he mut-tered, adjusting his tie. He glanced at his watch. "Time to go. By the way, the PM is sending along his niece. He said the two of you attended the same boarding school. Christina Whitestone.''

''Briefly,'' Erin said, recalling that Christina had been kicked out of boarding school for sneaking out at night to meet boys. Christina had been wilder than a March hare. She probably planned to seduce Daniel and have her wicked way with him. Or worse yet, marry him. Erin's stomach churned with jealousy.

''What do you know about her?'' Daniel asked, striding from his quarters.

That she's a slut, Erin thought. She bit her tongue, then sucked in a quick breath. ''I don't really know her well. We didn't attend the same boarding school very long, sir.''

Daniel stopped abruptly and studied Erin. ''What do you know about her? And I'd like the truth,'' he demanded. ''I have enough trouble knowing whom I can trust at the palace without wondering about the PM's niece.''

''I am truly not well acquainted with her. I only know her by reputation,'' Erin said, trying to take the high road.

Daniel arched an eyebrow. ''And her reputation is…?''

''Loose,'' Erin finally said.

His lips twitched, and his eyes glimmered with amusement. ''How refreshing,'' he said and continued down the hallway. ''I thought you were going to tell me she was interested in political espionage.''

"I'm quite sure political espionage is the last thing on Christina's mind," she said, and rounded the corner to the foyer. Erin immediately spotted Christina decked out in a dress that skimmed over every voluptuous curve. Seeing Daniel, the woman lifted her red lips into a sexually welcoming smile and gave a curtsey that gave His Majesty a perfect view of her enhanced cleavage.

Erin prayed her skin wasn't turning green as grass.

Eleven

With the exception of Christina's constant shrill laughter, Daniel's visit to the first farm couldn't have gone better. Erin noticed how he allowed the farmer to bow in respect, then Daniel was quick to show his own respect by shaking hands and asking questions as the entourage toured the damaged property.

Just as everyone prepared to leave, the farmer expressed his gratitude to his neighbors for donating materials and muscle for the barn-raising. As soon as the farmer mentioned it, Erin immediately knew what Daniel planned to do.

"Can I help?" Daniel asked.

The farmer gaped at him, embarrassed by the generous offer. "I can't—" The man shook his head in dismay. "Sir, I couldn't possibly—"

"My father made sure I could swing a hammer with the best of them. One more pair of hands will get the job done that much faster," he said and began removing his jacket.

Erin immediately went to his side. "Are you sure, sir?" she asked in a low voice, accepting his coat as he handed it to her.

"Very," he said, ditching his tie and unfastening a few of his shirt buttons. "I told you a suit was ridiculous."

Anthony Muller leaned closer. "Sir, we wouldn't want you to get hurt."

Daniel did a double take. "I realize that's your gentle way of telling me to avoid the embarrassment of hitting myself with the hammer. But I think I can manage. Tell the others if they want to join in and help, the palace will cover the dry-cleaning bills."

Christina and some of the aides watched in slack-jawed amazement as the new king joined the humble farmers in a barn-raising. Photographers snapped shot after shot. Erin joined a few of the farmers' wives in serving fruit juice and water.

The farmers were working on the roof while Daniel downed a glass of water. Sweat gleamed down his throat, and his white shirt was nearly transparent against his corded muscles.

Erin stared at him and felt her mouth go bone dry. She heard a cry and looked up in time to see a ham-

mer falling from the roof and heading straight for
Daniel. Still holding her tray, she clumsily lurched
forward to push Daniel aside. Everything happened
at once. She lifted one hand to deflect the falling
hammer, while the other firmly clutched the tray.
Her aim fell awry and the hammer's handle hit her
on the head. Pain reverberated through her head.

"Erin!" Daniel said.

Her vision went black for a second. She felt her
hands go slack. "The tray." Her head throbbed. She
wobbled on her feet, then suddenly felt herself air-
borne.

Her vision slowly cleared, and she looked up to
see Daniel frowning down at her and swearing.

"Did I drop the tray?" she whispered, wincing
from the pain.

He rolled his eyes and swore again. Seconds
passed and they were surrounded by farmers and
aides. A palace security man pulled her from Daniel's arms and carried her to a limousine. Erin
blinked at the dizzying effect of his movements.

Daniel appeared in the limo doorway, his gaze
searching hers. "How are you?"

"I'm fine, sir," Erin said, hurting, but not enough
to escape a feeling of total humiliation. "I suppose
I'm not a very good catcher. Another one of those
things I didn't learn in boarding school."

Daniel didn't smile. "What about your head?"

She gingerly touched her head and felt a goose

egg forming. "It's nothing," she lied. "Just a little bruise. Sorry for the fuss."

Daniel reached down to touch her head. "That feels like a knot to me. I'm sending you back to see the palace doctor."

Erin felt her cheeks heat with embarrassment. "That's totally unnecessary, sir," she insisted.

Daniel ignored her and turned his attention to the guard. "Take her back and make sure the doctor sees her."

"As you wish, sir," the guard said.

Daniel closed the door on her protests, and it occurred to her that he was enjoying his newfound ability to issue orders more quickly than she would have dreamed.

After the return drive to the palace, Erin endured an evaluation by the palace doctor. She was ordered to take her dinner in her room and rest. She was told she would be awakened every few hours. She groused to herself that she was being treated like a child, but fell asleep with the light on before eight o'clock.

Hours later a sound woke her from her sleep. She lifted her head and saw the outline of a man next to her bed. Fear raced through her, and she opened her mouth to scream, but panic froze her vocal cords.

"It's me. Daniel," the shadow said, moving closer so she could make out his face.

Her heart still hammering, Erin sagged with relief. "You scared me half to death."

"Fair is fair. You did the same to me this afternoon when you decided to have a head-on collision with a hammer," he told her, his voice softly chiding.

Erin sighed. "Well, I couldn't allow it to hit you," she said. "And I had nowhere to set the tray."

Daniel chuckled, and the sound evoked a ripple of pleasure over her nerve endings. "You have trouble letting things go."

She closed her eyes and covered her forehead with her hand. "It's that training I told you about. Though you would think they could have taught me to dodge a falling hammer or to whistle."

She felt his hand cover hers on her forehead, and the sensation was so comforting she held her breath. Oh, heavens, how she'd missed his touch.

"How's your head, really?"

"Fine," she said in a quiet voice. If she remained perfectly still, maybe he would stay a little longer.

"Thank you for catching the hammer," he said, sifting his fingers through her hair. "We're even now."

She peeked up at him through her fingers. "How are we even?"

"I helped you dodge a bullet. You helped me dodge a hammer."

Erin shook her head. "The hammer's head most likely wouldn't have killed you."

"Why didn't you tell me Christina had the most annoying laugh?"

Erin couldn't resist a smile. "I think most men don't listen to her as much as they look at her other...assets." Erin paused. "The prime minister is probably hoping you'll view her as a marriage prospect. Although she's—" Erin paused, searching for the most polite description "—extremely experienced, she has an excellent pedigree. You could do worse," she said dutifully and wondered why the whole discussion left a bad taste in her mouth.

Daniel lifted her hand to his lips. "Why are we talking about Christina?"

She slid him a sideways, accusing glance. "You brought her up."

He sank down on the bed beside her, searching her face. "I don't know what I'm going to do with you," he muttered. "You betray me, then save me from a hammer."

A knot formed in Erin's throat. "I didn't intend to betray you," she said, but he covered her lips with his finger and shook his head.

"Don't start," he said, his eyes moody and turbulent.

Erin's heart sank. She could see that he still struggled with his hurt and anger. "Will you ever be able to forgive me?" she whispered.

He looked at her for a long moment, rubbing his finger over her mouth. Finally, he nodded. "I'll be able to forgive you," he said. "But trust is another matter."

Erin knew she had lost something very very precious.

His gaze wrapped around her, and she felt a strange power surge between them. "Do you feel it?" she asked.

He nodded and lowered his mouth to hers. Erin closed her eyes and inhaled his scent, felt the texture of his lips against hers. She opened to his insistent pressure, wanting to please, to heal. She wondered if it was possible to love him so much on the outside that he felt it on the inside too.

His tongue tangled with hers and she lifted her hands to slide through his thick hair. His kiss grew more ardent. He slid his hands over the tiny straps of her nightgown, then rubbed his thumbs over the upper edge of her breasts.

Erin immediately felt her nipples tighten.

"I should stop," he said, pulling slightly away. "Your head must be hurting."

Erin bit her lip at the mix of arousal and passion plunging through her. "It's not," she said and pushed her hands through his open shirt to his muscular chest. "Are you aware that you drove all the women crazy with your broad shoulders and muscles today?"

His mouth lifted in a slight grin. "Can't say that thought crossed my mind. I didn't know you noticed my body."

Erin swallowed a groan. "That's the most ridiculous thing you've ever said."

"No, it's not," he said. "You've never said a word about my body."

Erin rolled her eyes. "Well, I suppose you could say I've revealed my opinion more by actions than words."

His lids lowered to a sexy half-mast. "What's your opinion right now?" he asked, his words both a challenge and an invitation.

Erin's heart pounded against her rib cage. "Come close and let me show you," she said, and she did.

She kissed her way down his chest, dragged her tongue over his belly and would have gone further, but he stopped her and took a little pleasure of his own. He suckled the tips of her breasts until she arched toward him, and slid his hand between her thighs to find her wet and swollen.

Murmuring his approval, he pushed her legs apart and thrust inside her. Erin sighed at the feeling of delicious fullness. He gave her seconds to grow accustomed to him, then began a rhythm that took away her mind and breath.

She craved every possible intimacy with him. He drove her higher and higher until she clenched around him. He shuddered, then pulled himself from her at the last moment before his release.

Erin immediately felt the loss. They'd been so close. Her breath was harsh with exertion, as was

his. Confused, she stared up at him. "Why did
you—"

"I didn't have any protection for you," he managed, his look as tumultuous as if he were fighting
his own set of demons concerning her. He closed
his eyes, then shifted away from her, pulling the
sheet over her. "I shouldn't have done this," he
muttered.

His words cut her. She understood his disappoint-
ment in her, his anger. She even understood his dis-
enchantment. But she couldn't bear his regret. "You
should go," she whispered, refusing to give in to
tears. "You shouldn't be here."

She felt him look down at her, but she didn't meet
his gaze. "Go to sleep, Erin."

She waited for him to leave, then buried her face
in her pillow and sobbed. Overwhelming despera-
tion shook her. She knew she couldn't look at him
again. There was only one thing to do: she had to
leave.

Daniel avoided Erin for the next two days. He was
so busy it wasn't difficult to do. He resented his
weakness for her. He shouldn't have made love to
her the other night, but he'd been unable to resist
his need for her. Even now, he struggled with the
itchy need to see her. Three days was too long. He
kept his eyes open for her throughout the day, but
didn't see her.

During a formal business dinner, in a quiet voice,

he casually mentioned her to his chief of staff, Anthony Muller.

Anthony shrugged. "She resigned the day before yesterday, sir."

"Excuse me?"

Anthony must have perceived Daniel's displeasure. He frowned. "I apologize, sir. I thought you knew. She moved out and took a position with a local tour agency."

"Tour agency?" Daniel echoed. "Didn't she move in with her father?"

Anthony shook his head. "No. She took a small apartment at the far end of town. The tour agency is quite successful. They cater to businessmen, lead tours into the mountains and host beach parties."

Daniel felt his blood roar to his head. "Beach parties with businessmen? It sounds like a damn escort service to me"

Anthony shifted uncomfortably. "To my knowledge, sir, they're completely legitimate."

Daniel took a calming breath. "I'd like you to find out her schedule. I also want to know her new address," he said. "Immediately," he added and couldn't force down one more bite.

Immediately after Daniel finished the interminable meal one hour later, he received all his information and he didn't like most of it. Erin was apparently hosting a bonfire at the beach this evening. The very thought of her with all those men made him sick.

He wondered why she hadn't returned to her father, though he suspected Erin and her father were no longer on speaking terms. That probably hurt her to no end. It had been so obvious that she had wanted a close relationship with her father. She had wanted it badly, yet she'd given in to her feelings for Daniel.

The knowledge did strange things to his heart. Lord, what a mess. The truth of the matter was that if she'd been sent to him with a duplicitous scheme, she'd done a rotten job pulling it off. In fact, she hadn't pulled off what her father had apparently asked of her. Daniel wondered if that was why she wasn't living with the man and felt a surprising rush of protectiveness.

He thought of the sweet way she'd given him her innocence and her terror when the bullet grazed his forehead. He remembered the terrible hurt on her face when he'd rejected her, and recalled her determination to make his private quarters feel like a home.

He wanted her back.

He gave Anthony his instructions as the two men sat in the parked limo.

"Sir, I cannot recommend you making an unannounced appearance at the bonfire party tonight," the chief of staff said bluntly.

"Thank you for your recommendation. Have you informed security where I want to go?" Daniel asked, adjusting his tie and red sash.

"Yes, and the security chief is most displeased."

"He'll get over it," Daniel said.

Anthony sighed. "Sir, are you certain you want to do this?"

"Never more," Daniel said and knocked back some liquid courage from the limo's bar while security did their thing.

If Erin had to dance with one more man, she was going to scream. The bonfire blazed in the wind, and the sound of the ocean was muted behind the string quartet playing lively island music.

She bared her teeth in a smile as the music blessedly stopped, and stole a quick glance at her watch. Forty-five more minutes and she could return to her apartment and collapse.

Although thoughts of Daniel haunted her day and night, moving into her small apartment had been liberating. Now that she was employed, she was neither dependent nor obligated to anyone but herself. If she still ached with a terrible loss, she refused to dwell on it.

The music began again and another man approached her with a smile. "Dance?"

Swallowing a sigh, she allowed him to take her hand. Halfway through the song, the partying crowd began pointing down the beach. Erin looked over her shoulder, but her partner spun her around so she couldn't see.

Before she knew it, she looked beyond the customer and found Daniel staring at her. Her heart stuttering, she immediately fumbled and stepped on the customer's foot.

The man grunted.

Daniel tapped the man's shoulder, and the customer threw him a look of irritation. "This is my dance. I've been waiting all evening."

A palace guard stepped beside the man. "I would like to introduce His Majesty, Daniel Connelly, King of Altaria."

The customer's eyes nearly popped out of his head. "His Majesty!" He whirled around. "Are you the king?"

"I am," Daniel said, and extended his hand. "And you are?"

"Bob," the man said, clearly bowled over. "Bob Fuller."

"It's a pleasure to meet you, Bob. Are you enjoying Altaria?"

"Oh, yeah. It's great. The weather, the beach, the women," Bob slid his gaze toward Erin.

Daniel's cordial smile stiffened. "Would you mind if I finish this dance?"

Bob looked at Erin. "No. Go ahead. I'll catch her again later."

Daniel immediately took her into his arms. "Over my dead body," he muttered to himself. He looked at Erin. "What in hell are you doing?"

Erin's mind was spinning. "Working. This is my job."

"No, it isn't. Your job is at the palace," Daniel

said, his jaw as firm as granite.

"I quit," Erin said, her heart bumping against her rib cage.

He looked as if he were counting to ten to remain under control. "I'm talking about a different position."

"What?" she asked wryly. "Royal dog walker and pooper scooper?"

He sucked in a quick breath, and Erin got the uncomfortable sense that she had just crossed his line in the sand.

"We need to talk," he said. "You're coming with me."

"I can't," she protested. "I need this job."

"You're quitting this job," he told her.

"I don't think so."

"I know so," he said, and shocked the spit out of her by picking her up in his arms and carrying her. A roar of chuckles followed after them.

"What on earth are you doing?" she hissed as he trudged to a black limousine. "If the press gets wind of this, everyone will think you're crazy."

"Then there's only one solution," he said, dumping her into the back seat.

"What is that?" she demanded.

"I'll tell you when we get to the palace."

Erin crossed her arms mutinously over her chest during the short ride to the palace. He had gone entirely too far this time. She just knew she would get sacked for this, and it was all his fault.

As soon as the limo stopped, Daniel exited the car and came to her side to collect her. Erin refused to budge. "I want to return to my apartment. You have no right to force me into the palace," she told him.

He exhaled and softly swore. "Well, if you're going to be difficult," he said, and tossed her over his shoulder.

Erin's blood rushed to her head. "Put me down at once," she insisted, her voice rising. "Put me down. You're embarrassing both of us."

"I'm not embarrassed," he said, hauling her through the grand foyer.

"Put me down," she said, feeling her slim shred of control slipping through her fingers. "Put me—" She hiccuped. "Oh, look what you've—" she hiccuped "—done. You gave me the hiccups."

Still carrying her, he lowered her into a slightly more respectable position and looked down at her. "I want to give you hiccups for the rest of your life."

Confused and near tears, Erin hiccuped again. "What are you talking about?" she asked before another spasm shook her.

"I want to marry you."

Erin blinked. Her breath and heart seemed to stop. A second later, she hiccuped. "You can't marry me," she whispered. "You don't trust me."

"Change my mind," he dared her. "I'm almost there."

She bit her lip and felt another hiccup. "I can't imagine having any significant influence over a man as strong-minded as you."

"Then you need to do something about your imagination."

Erin fell silent. With the exception of her hiccups. She felt as if the world had been turned upside down. Or turned upright. She stared at Daniel and wondered if a person could burst from hope and love.

"I want you with me all the time, Erin," Daniel said. "Hell, I'll even get you a poodle."

She blinked. A poodle was the last thing on her mind.

His eyes were drop-dead serious. "When I look at you, I want things I've never wanted before. I want to love and protect you the rest of my life. I want to raise children with you. I want to lead Altaria into a great new age with you by my side. But most of all, Erin, I want to live every day of my life with you." His nostrils flared. "Damn it, Erin. Say something."

"Yes," she whispered and took her heart in her hands and gave it to Daniel's safekeeping. She wondered how she could have traveled her whole life and found her home in this man's eyes.

"Yes," he echoed as if he didn't quite trust her breathless response.

"Yes," she said with all the conviction flooding through her. "I will marry you. I will have your children. I will stand by your side." She lifted her hand to his strong jaw. "I will love you forever," she said and knew beyond the shadow of a doubt that she would.

Epilogue

A week later Erin and Daniel were married in an outdoor ceremony on the palace lawn. The royal advisors had protested the speed, but Daniel had been adamant. They would have to postpone an extended honeymoon until after Daniel's coronation, but Erin didn't mind. She knew the ongoing investigation into the deaths of King Thomas and Prince Marc weighed heavily on Daniel's mind and heart, and he wouldn't rest until the murderers were found and punished.

Despite her ambivalence, Daniel insisted that Erin's father attend the ceremony. He was determined that she would experience the feeling of family she'd missed her entire life. There'd been a moment or two of awkwardness, but Erin sensed her father wished for a genuine reconciliation as much as she did.

After the ceremony and reception, which was internationally televised, she and Daniel escaped to Dunemere, the Rosemere family's beach house. Erin was certain she and Daniel would take refuge in the two-story, shingled wood frame house on many future occasions. The hideaway overflowed with flowers from Daniel's family and the joy between she and Daniel. Erin had never dreamed she could be so completely cherished.

She looked down at her naked husband lying replete from their lovemaking. His urgency had taken her by surprise at the same time that it turned her on. It was as if he'd needed to claim her as his wife.

"I love you," he said, the power of his feelings glowing in his eyes.

Her heart swelled with emotion. "I feel like crying every time you tell me."

He gently smiled. "Better than hiccups?"

She laughed. "I suppose," she said, and traced his strong jaw. She thought about the vows they'd just made. "Sometimes I still don't understand, why me? Why would you want to marry me?"

He glanced away for a moment. "From the first moment I met you, something told me I could trust you."

Erin's stomach tightened, and she closed her eyes. She still hated to think of how hurt he had been.

"Look at me," he told her, kissing her lightly. "Even after I heard that awful conversation with your father, there was a part of me that still trusted you. That part was right," he told her. "I trust you with my life, with my future."

Her eyes welled with tears. "Do you realize you've made me the happiest woman in the world?"

"Erin," he said, with passion and promise in his eyes, "I'm just getting started."

*   *   *   *   *

DYNASTIES: THE CONNELLYS

King Thomas Rosemere (d) m. Queen Lucinda (d)

Sonia Anton

Prince Marc Rosemere (d)

Princess Emma Rosemere m. Grant Connelly

Tobias Connelly m. Lilly

Hannah Barnett

Angie Donahue

④ Chance Barnett-Connelly•

⑤ Douglas Barnett-Connelly•

Twins

③ Princess Catherine Rosemere•

① Daniel Connelly (heir apparent) m. Erin Lawrence

⑪ Rafe Connelly

⑦ Alexandra Connelly

④ Justin Connelly

② Brett Connelly

⑧ Drew Connelly 1st m. Talia Van Dorn (d)

Amanda Connelly

Twins

⑨ Tara Connelly

⑫ Maggie Connelly

⑩ Seth Connelly•

① *Tall, Dark & Royal*
② *Maternally Yours*
③ *The Sheikh Takes a Bride*
④ *The SEAL's Surrender*
⑤ *Plain Jane & Doctor Dad*
⑥ *And the Winner Gets...Married!*
⑦ *The Royal & the Runaway Bride*
⑧ *The Secret Baby Bond*
⑨ *His E-Mail Order Wife*
⑩ *Cinderella's Convenient Husband*
⑪ *Expecting...and In Danger*
⑫ *Cherokee Marriage Dare*

Symbols:
- - - - Affair
• Child of an Affair
(d) Deceased

Look for the story of
Brett Connelly and Elena Delgado in
MATERNALLY YOURS
by Kathie DeNosky
Book 2 (SD1418) in the
exciting new miniseries,
Dynasties: The Connellys,
from Silhouette Desire
On sale February 2002
For a sneak preview, turn the page...

One

Elena Delgado pressed a shaky hand to her stomach, took a deep breath and slowly got to her feet. She closed her eyes and leaned against the side of the rest room stall. The nausea wasn't supposed to last all day. If it was, they would have called it something besides morning sickness. But she'd been ill almost from the instant the test stick turned blue.

She didn't mind in the least. She'd gladly go through whatever it took to complete this pregnancy successfully. She bit her lower lip and took another deep breath. This was her last hope of having her own child, of holding it and loving it with every fiber of her being—she simply couldn't afford another trip to the sperm bank. Not financially. Not emotionally.

When her stomach finally settled down, she pulled the door open and walked over to the vanity. The click of her black medium-heeled pumps striking the tiled floor echoed through the empty room. She shivered at the hollow loneliness of the sound.

Tears filled her eyes as she looked at herself in the mirror above the bank of sinks. She'd been alone all of her life. So why was she feeling so lonely now?

Disgusted with herself, Elena jerked paper towels from the dispenser on the wall and held them under the faucet, then pressed the cool wetness to her flushed cheeks. Her unstable emotions had to be caused by the hormonal changes from her pregnancy. That was the only thing it could be.

Otherwise Elena Delgado never cried. Ever.

She finished wiping away the last of the tears, draped her coat over her arm, then checked her watch. Groaning, she quickly grabbed her shoulder bag, said a silent prayer that her queasy stomach would remain calm for the next hour and walked out into the stylish reception of Connelly Tower.

Heading for the elevators, she shook her head. She hated to be late for anything. It was rude and inconsiderate to keep people waiting. She shifted from one foot to the other as she impatiently waited for an elevator. Just one more slowdown in a day that had been filled with a series of delays and frustrations.

She'd awakened this morning to find that some-

time during the night the ancient furnace in her
building had finally given up the fight against Chicago's cold, hard winters and died. It had taken her
twice as long to get ready for work because she
couldn't stop shivering. Then she'd gone out to find
that her car wouldn't start, forcing her to walk six
blocks in the frigid February temperature to catch
the L.

The polished brass doors of the elevator finally
swished open and Elena hurriedly stepped inside.
She pressed the button to the seventeenth floor, and
as it began to move, she closed her eyes against a
wave of nausea. Express elevators should be out-
lawed, she decided as the rapid ascent played havoc
with her already iffy stomach.

When it eased to a stop a few seconds later and
the doors opened, she stepped out into the plushly
carpeted corridor on shaky legs. After she met with
Brett Connelly to arrange interviews with the rest of
the Connelly family, she would go home and spend
the weekend trying to feel human again. But when
she left, she would take the stairs down.

Brett Connelly tapped the highly polished surface
of his mahogany desk with his fountain pen. Glancing at his watch for the third time in as many
minutes, he resumed staring out the window at the
early-evening shadows covering Lake Michigan. He
hated to be kept waiting. If the detective investigat-
ing the attempted murder of his older brother, Dan-

iel, didn't show up damned quick, Brett was calling it a day. The Babe didn't like him to be late getting home from work. In fact, he'd be lucky if she didn't destroy some of his things to get back at him. She'd done that several times already.

The intercom on the corner of his desk suddenly buzzed, interrupting his thoughts. "Yes, Fiona?"

"Your five-thirty appointment has arrived, Mr. Connelly."

"Thank you. Send her in." As an afterthought, he added, "If you'd like, you can leave now."

"Thank you, Mr. Connelly. I'll see you Monday. Have a nice weekend."

"You, too, Fiona."

Seconds later his office door opened, and a young woman with shoulder-length, tawny-brown hair walked into the room. Brett couldn't keep from staring. This was the hotshot detective from the Special Investigative Unit of the Chicago Police Department?

Whoa, baby! He'd been expecting some middle-aged battle-ax who looked like a man and had a hard-as-nails attitude. Instead they'd sent a petite woman who had to be somewhere in her midtwenties and could put beauty queens to shame with her looks. He made a mental note to call and thank his father for assigning him the task of liaison between his family and the police.

Brett rose to his feet as his gaze zeroed in on her

left hand to see if she wore a wedding band. She didn't.

Sending a silent thank-you to the powers that be, he rounded the desk, treated her to his most charming smile—the smile that had kept his social calendar filled since his sophomore year in high school—and extended his hand. "I'm Brett Connelly, Vice President of Public Relations. And you are?"

She quickly shook his hand but didn't return his smile. "I'm SIU Detective Elena Delgado. Sorry I'm late, Mr. Connelly."

She wasn't offering an explanation for her tardiness, and Brett wasn't asking for one. He was too preoccupied with the tingling sensation running from his palm, up his arm and warming his chest.

"Since we'll be working so closely together, please call me Brett, Ms. Delgado," he said, rubbing his thumb over the silky skin on the back of her hand.

She dropped his hand, and the look she gave him indicated that she hadn't been the least bit affected by his never-fail smile or his touch. At least not the way he'd been affected by hers.

"Shall we get down to business, Mr. Connelly?" she asked politely.

Silhouette *Desire*

presents

DYNASTIES: THE CONNELLYS

A brand-new miniseries about the Connellys of Chicago, a wealthy, powerful American family tied by blood to the royal family of the island kingdom of Altaria. They're wealthy, powerful and rocked by scandal, betrayal…and passion!

Look for a whole year of glamorous and utterly romantic tales in 2002:

Silhouette®

Where love comes alive™

Visit Silhouette at www.eHarlequin.com

SDDYN02

Silhouette —

where love comes alive—online...

eHARLEQUIN.com

SINTA1R2

**You are invited to enter the
exclusive, masculine
world of the...**

**Silhouette Desire's powerful miniseries
features five wealthy Texas bachelors—all
members of the state's most prestigious club—
who set out to uncover a traitor in their midst...
and discover their true loves!**

THE MILLIONAIRE'S PREGNANT BRIDE
by Dixie Browning
February 2002 (SD #1420)

HER LONE STAR PROTECTOR
by Peggy Moreland
March 2002 (SD #1426)

TALL, DARK...AND FRAMED?
by Cathleen Galitz
April 2002 (SD #1433)

THE PLAYBOY MEETS HIS MATCH
by Sara Orwig
May 2002 (SD #1438)

THE BACHELOR TAKES A WIFE
by Jackie Merritt
June 2002 (SD #1444)

Available at your favorite retail outlet.

Where love comes alive™